"I'm su
we'll j

MW01077526

Vᴀʟʟᴇʏ ᴏғ ᴛʜᴇ Sʜᴀᴅᴏᴡ

For eight years, Baojia and Natalie have pursued their goals: family, career, friendship, and love—trying to carve out an ordinary life in an immortal world. And for eight years they've been mostly successful save for a world-bending adventure every now and then.

Except that their life was never ordinary. It was never going to be.

Natalie and Baojia might have made plans, but when ordinary life comes crashing down, they'll have to turn to the family they have chosen—vampire and human—for help keeping their world together.

Five couples, four kids, three weeks, two paths… and a partridge in a pear tree? Return to the Elemental World for a Christmas reunion of old friends and forever loves.

For Natalie Ellis, it's time to come home.

Valley of the Shadow is a novella in the Elemental World series by *USA Today* bestseller Elizabeth Hunter, author of the Elemental Mysteries, the Irin Chronicles, and Love Stories on 7th and Main.

VALLEY OF THE SHADOW
AN ELEMENTAL WORLD NOVELLA

ELIZABETH HUNTER

Cover: Damonza
Content Editor: Amy Cissell, Cissell Ink
Line Editor: Anne Victory
Proofreader: Linda, Victory Editing

Recurve Press LLC
PO Box 4034
Visalia, California 93278
USA

This book is dedicated to every
Natalie and Baojia fan
who has asked over the years...
So what happens?
Thanks for being so patient.

"I would be giving up everything to love you. I wanted a family. I wanted a normal life. I wanted what my parents had no matter how it ended. Do you know what loving you would mean for me? For my life?"

"Yes. *Love me anyway.*"

— BLOOD AND SAND

CHAPTER ONE

*B*aojia lived his immortal life from sundown to midnight. He and Natalie had decided as a family that midnight was as late as two small children could be allowed to stay awake, even if they had a nontraditional school schedule and slept until noon. Though his security work sometimes interrupted, the primary focus of his life from sundown to midnight was his children and his wife.

He carried his squirming daughter under one arm and nudged his son with the other. "Bed."

Jake yawned loudly. "I'm not ti-ired."

"Clearly." He mussed the boy's dark brown hair. "We can finish the game tomorrow."

"But not until you wake up," Jake whined. "I don't want to wait that long."

His daughter, Sarah, did her best impression of a boiled spaghetti noodle and flipped backward in his arms.

"It's good to want things." Baojia wrangled Sarah

upright. "It teaches you patience. Don't play dead, Monkey. You're going to hit your head."

Sarah's lively brown eyes were not tired in the least. "I'm not playing dead. I'm playing vampire!" She patted her father's cheek. "Let me see, let me see."

He forced himself to snarl and allowed his fangs to fall. "Rawr."

Sarah squealed in delight and nearly twisted out of his arms again. "Rawr, rawr, rawr!"

Jake looked up with adoration. "I'm gonna have really big fangs when I grow up."

"That"—Baojia nudged him into his room—"is a very mature decision that you cannot make until you are very old."

"How old?" Jake hopped into his bed.

Baojia slung Sarah over his shoulder to keep her from crawling out of his arms. She truly was their monkey. She crawled and climbed on everything in sight. "Hmm... let me think."

Jake wasn't budging. He crossed his arms over his skinny seven-year-old chest. It was a gesture he'd recently begun copying from Baojia. "When can I decide I want to be a vampire?"

Baojia went with his gut. "When you're forty-seven."

Jake's mouth dropped. "What? No way, Dad. I don't want to be an old man."

"Forty-seven isn't old."

"It's *really* old." Sarah grabbed Baojia's head and pulled herself up to sit on his shoulder. "That's almost a hundred, Dad."

He laughed low and long. Nothing made him laugh more than his children. They were the light and life of his eternity, and words could not express how grateful for them he was.

Even when they were being restless.

"Bedtime, Jake."

He swung Sarah onto his back and sat on the edge of Jake's bed while they said good-night prayers. It was a habit Natalie had begun with both the children, and while Baojia wasn't religious, he appreciated the habit of gratitude it engendered.

"And thank you for our house," Jake said. "And thank you for my bike."

"And my bike too," Sarah whispered.

"Thank you for Sarah's baby bike."

"Jake." Baojia's voice was a warning.

"And thank you for fishing. And thank you for Ariel and Miss Olivia."

Baojia murmured, "Wrap it up."

His son could be very grateful. For close to an hour if he didn't want to go to bed.

"And thank you for Uncle Lucien and Auntie Mak and for Cousin Carina and also for Butch. Amen." Jake finished his prayers and opened his eyes, his lips pressed together.

Baojia raised an eyebrow. "Butch?"

"He's out there, Dad. We just haven't found him yet."

Jake was bound and determined to have a dog. He'd been begging for two years. Natalie and Baojia had resisted. They already had enough people in and out of their house simply to help take care of two active children. A dog seemed like another thing to keep track of.

"I know it." Jake yawned loudly. "When Butch finds us, you'll know too."

"I'll keep my eyes open." He bent over and kissed Jake's forehead. "Good night. I love you."

"I love you too!" Sarah sang. She giggled when Baojia stood and swung her from his back into his arms.

"Love you, Dad." Jake punched his pillows to get them exactly as he wanted. "Tell Mom I hope she's feeling better."

"I will." He held Sarah in place as she tried to crawl up his shoulder and onto his head. "Sweet dreams."

He walked out of Jake's room and into Sarah's. A bathroom connected the two rooms, but while Jake's bedroom was decorated plainly with dark green trim and dinosaurs scattered everywhere, Sarah's was an explosion of purple.

Purple curtains. Purple bed. Purple-painted monkeys crawling along the top of each wall. Baojia tossed Sarah onto her bed and smiled when the little girl erupted in giggles.

"Do it again." She held out her arms.

"No." He sat on the edge of her bed and tried to settle her down. "I'll read you a book, and then you need to sleep."

"I want Mama to read it."

"Mama is not feeling well," Baojia said, "so we're letting her sleep."

Sarah pouted. "I want to go say good night."

"You already did that."

"I want a glass of water."

Baojia pointed to the water bottle by her bed. "Done."

"I want…" She huffed out a breath. "I want… a stuffie."

"Sarah." Baojia stood and gave her the look she had to recognize. "Seriously?"

Sarah looked at the line of stuffed animals decorating her bed and shrugged helplessly. "Someone is missing."

He stood and watched her from the corner of his eye as he walked over to the hammock of stuffed animals in the corner. "Lion?" It was an adorable fluffy thing that had no basis in reality, but she loved it.

Sarah shook her head.

"Unicorn?"

Eyes wide, she shook her head again.

"Snake?"

She considered it, but it was a firm headshake. Not the snake, but he was on the right track. His smallest child had a warped sense of humor and a fondness for the macabre.

Not unlike her mother.

Baojia lifted another one. "Bat?"

She cocked her head and considered it. "Mmmm. No."

Baojia sighed and picked up the one he would have grabbed first if he hadn't wanted to go through the mock trial Sarah loved so much.

"Vampire?"

Eyes wide, Sarah grinned and held out her arms.

Baojia sighed and tossed her the ridiculous joke his wife had bought the Christmas before. It was a stuffed cartoon vampire with a purple cape and felt fangs. It looked like it belonged on a cereal box.

Sarah absolutely loved it. Just as Natalie had known she would.

You married an evil, evil woman.

"Okay. Book, then bed." Baojia sat next to his little girl as she snuggled under the purple blanket, hugging the ridiculous vampire and sucking her thumb. "And remind me what the silly vampire's name is?"

Sarah took her thumb out of her mouth. "Giovanni."

Baojia smiled. "That's right."

He pulled his shirt off before he slipped into bed next to his wife.

"Hmm?" Natalie rolled toward him, her face pale and her long red hair piled on top of her head. "Hey, handsome. Kids in bed?"

"Yes." He scooted next to her and pulled her into his chest. "How are you feeling?"

"I'm just overtired." She yawned and snuggled in. "I had those two deadlines last week, and I've been running on empty."

"You need to sleep more." He stroked a hand over her hair. "Maybe the kids' schedule—"

"Shh." She put a finger over his lips. "The schedule is fine. I'm fine. Just working too much. Thanks for putting the kids to bed."

"It was my turn anyway." He kissed her hand. "Did you want to sleep more?"

"Maybe." She drifted a little, still drowsy. Her hand traced the lines of muscle on his chest. "Give me a minute."

If she wanted to sleep, Baojia didn't mind lying with her. His wife was his favorite person. He could sit all night just listening to her heart beating and hearing her breathe.

He loved watching Natalie, seeing the changes in her face and her body as the years passed. They'd been together over eight years, and Baojia felt the privilege of witnessing her mortal years because she had chosen *him* to be a permanent part of her life.

Natalie had transformed during pregnancy, a fascinating and frightening time for a vampire unaccustomed to change. Her belly swelled and marks appeared on her skin. Her lips and breasts were fuller. Her feet grew bigger. Her dark red hair had thickened, and even her heart sounded different. Her blood tasted richer, and he had to be very careful when he took her vein. He'd tried to abstain, but she'd put her foot down.

During the first pregnancy, he'd been more than a little alarmed. Then it happened again, and he wasn't alarmed, but their three-year-old son had been.

Family life, Baojia had decided, was the greatest and most unexpected adventure.

"Is Sarah sleeping?" Natalie murmured.

"Hopefully."

"With her vampire?"

He grunted. "Yes."

She let out an evil laugh. "I'm going to get Sadia one for her next birthday."

Baojia smiled. "What an excellent idea." He loosened her hair and began playing with it.

"Ugh." She batted his hand. "It's dirty. I need to wash it."

"I don't care if your hair is dirty." He spread it out and feathered it over his skin. "It's still sexy."

She lifted her head from his chest and wriggled her eyebrows. "My dirty hair is sexy?"

He ran his hand down her shoulder, under her arm,

and along the side of her breast. "Everything about you is sexy."

"Mmmm." Her eyes turned from sleepy to playful. "I see someone doesn't want to leave the bed."

He smiled and scooted down so he could kiss her. "Why would I want to leave the bed when you're in it?"

She met his lips in a long, languid kiss, sighing into his mouth. "Don't know. Thought you might have…" She stroked her tongue out and flicked the tip over his already-extended fangs. "…work or something."

"Something." He sank into her kiss, ran his hand down her thigh, and hiked her leg over his hip. "I do have something… to do."

"Oh yeah?" She ran her hand along his nape, playing with the ends of his short hair, which needed to be trimmed. "What's that?"

"I need to debrief you about…" He traced the lace trim on her panties. "…something very important. This underwear has to go."

"Just the underwear?" She bit his chin. "I mean, I can leave the pajamas on, but you might have to get creative."

"Ha ha." He began tugging. "I could rip these off."

"You better not. This is my last clean pair of pj's."

She quickly shoved her sleep shorts and underwear down her legs, kicking them down to the foot of the bed. Baojia lifted her shirt up and teased her breasts, making her arch her back and sigh happily.

He was just pulling her shirt over her head when the door creaked open.

"Mom?"

Nooooo.

"You forgot to lock the door?" she hissed.

"Stay." Baojia poked his head up from the covers. "Sarah, go to bed."

"I'm thirsty."

"Uh-uh." His voice was sharp. "Bed. Now."

She pretended to sniff. "But I miss Mom."

Natalie shoved the tangled hair out of her face and lifted her head. "Sarah, honey, what did Dad say?"

"But—"

"I said good night to you earlier."

"But—"

"I'm gonna use amnis on her," Baojia muttered. "Don't think I won't."

"Shhh." Natalie was trying to bite back a laugh. "You are not." She raised her voice. "Sarah, I already said good night. You're not getting in bed with us. What did Dad say?"

Sarah sighed.

"What was that?"

"S' timefrbed," she mumbled. She let out one last pitiful sigh before she closed the door.

Baojia waited to hear her little feet walk back to her bedroom, shuffling the whole way. Her door creaked open. Shut. He could hear her muttering under her breath as she got back into bed.

He looked down at Natalie, whose lips and cheeks were still flushed. "We are the worst."

"The meanest parents ever."

He smiled and settled back down in bed. "Horrible and rotten."

"Come here." She hooked her arm around his neck. "Let me show you what I do to horrible, rotten, mean vampires as sexy as you."

"Hold that thought." He slipped out of bed. "And let me lock the door."

BAOJIA WOKE THE NEXT NIGHT IN THE SMALL ROOM THEY'D built into the farmhouse where they lived on the Northern California coast. He took a moment to orient himself, listening for the voices he expected beyond the thick cement walls of his day chamber. It had been built to withstand storms, earthquakes, explosive concussions, and gunfire. In it, there was a small bathroom and enough provisions for four humans to survive for thirty days.

His day chamber also doubled as their panic room, which was necessary when you were the senior security chief for the immortal in charge of the Pacific Northwest, much of Canada, Alaska, and a not-insignificant part of Russia.

Baojia listened for the expected sounds of life beyond the walls of his day chamber.

But the sounds were unexpected.

"Mom?" His son sounded scared.

"Are they awake yet?" It was the nanny, and her voice was panicked. "Natalie, would Baojia be awake yet? The sun is down. How about Lucien and Mak?"

He didn't wait another moment. Pulling on a pair of sweatpants, he unlocked the dead bolt that secured his room and rushed toward the voices, which were coming from the kitchen and dining area.

"Natalie?"

He forced himself to remain calm when he saw her lying on the kitchen floor. Sarah was crying. Jake was sitting next to his mother on the floor, and Ariel, their children's nanny, was on the phone.

She spotted him. "I'm on the phone with Lucien."

"Tell him to come." He bent down and looked in her face. Her eyes were open. She wasn't unconscious. "What happened?"

"Just…" Natalie tried shaking her head, but her pupils were abnormally dilated. She blinked. "Dizzy. I just got dizzy. I lay down on the floor so I wouldn't fall. That's all."

"Have you eaten today?"

"Had breakfast with the kids. Snack an hour ago. Something like that."

That should have been enough. He performed a basic physical exam. She didn't have a fever. Her skin was cool and clammy. "Jake, take Sarah into the family room."

"I wanna stay with Mama!" Sarah wailed.

"Sarah." Baojia gave her a steady look. "Mama is going to be fine. She's just a little sick. Remember when you got the flu and threw up last winter?"

Sarah stuck her thumb in her mouth and nodded.

"Mama is sick like you were." Mama was *not* sick like Sarah had been. Natalie had no fever. Her pulse was normal. Something else was going on. "I know it's scary when Mama gets sick," he continued, "but Uncle Lucien is going to come over and give her a checkup, so you and Jakey need to go play so there's room in the kitchen."

Ariel held out her hand. "Come on, guys. Let's go do a puzzle, okay?"

Jake was giving him suspicious eyes.

"Jake," Baojia said, "I need you to take care of Sarah."

"Okay." His voice was small. He stood and held his

hand out for his sister. "Come on, Monkey. Dad'll take care of Mom."

"Can I get up now?" Natalie's lips were pale. "I'm not dizzy anymore."

"Stay put." He put a hand on her cheek and spoke quietly. "Just… give me a break, okay, Red? Stay here until Lucien can examine you."

Red like firecrackers. Like chili peppers. Like her hair. Natalie didn't look like her nickname just then. She looked tired and wan and unwell.

Baojia clamped down on the creeping terror that lived in his heart. Every night he had to control his fear and pretend the world was a safe place. That he could keep the monsters at bay. That his children would be protected. He had to, or he would go insane. But as he knelt next to Natalie in the middle of the kitchen, the fear crept out and would not be contained.

Something was wrong with his wife.

CHAPTER TWO

"Okay." Natalie stared at the paper Lucien had handed her. "So *that* debate is over."

"I'm sorry," Lucien said. "I'm very sorry."

She took a deep breath and let it out slowly, her eyes never leaving the top page of the report. "This was always the plan. The debate has just been about when."

"It needs to be sooner," he said, "rather than later."

Natalie finally looked up into the face of the vampire who was her doctor and her friend. "How long?"

Lucien rubbed a thumb along his jaw. "Weeks, not months."

The reality of those words hit her right in the chest. She let out a hard breath, and the tears she'd been holding at bay started to leak out of her eyes. "Weeks?"

"New Year's at the very latest. Waiting any longer could mean that you're not in optimal health when you make the change."

"I'm not in optimal health right now, Lucien." Natalie

rubbed her eyes and wiped her cheeks. "I have…" She took a breath. "I have breast cancer."

"Yes, you do. You also have options. Traditional treatments for breast cancer are very good," he said. "The five-year survival rate for this type and stage is nearly ninety percent. If you want a referral to an oncologist, I will find you the very best. Money would be no object."

Because Lucien was the son of Saba, who was basically the queen of the vampire race and also richer than Croesus, which meant Lucien was rolling in money too. And with no human family left after thousands of years, he'd chosen Natalie, Baojia, and their kids as his own.

"Ninety percent success?"

"My best guess would be surgery followed by chemotherapy. But I'm not an oncologist."

Natalie looked back at her report. Two tumors hidden in the dense tissue of her left breast, right over her heart. "But after that? After five years, what are the chances the cancer will come back?"

"I can't tell you that."

"Is it genetic?"

"I don't know that either, but it might be worth taking a test. You're young."

Her mother hadn't lived much past forty, and Natalie was approaching that.

"I know what I want to do." She reached for his hand. "I want to go with plan V."

Lucien nodded. "That would be my first choice, but you know he'll be unhappy."

She sniffed. "Uh, he'll be happiest with me alive and still around for my children."

"You know you won't be able—"

"I know." She closed her eyes and tried not to think about the time she'd have to spend away from Jake and Sarah. "But treatment would mean I'd be sick and maybe gone too. Hospital visits. Nausea. And with all that, the odds of something going wrong and permanently damaging my health are greater, aren't they?"

"Chemotherapy, at its core, destroys your body to destroy the cancer. Radiation and surgery—"

"They all have risks." She closed the file. "This isn't a debate anymore. It's not a debate, Lucien. This just needs to happen."

Lucien nodded. "Unfortunately, I agree."

"Okay." She took a deep breath and flexed the knee that still ached first thing every morning. "I guess I'll be dealing with that for eternity."

"We don't know how turning would affect your mobility or your joints."

She waved a hand. "Not important."

Natalie mentally began to construct how she'd present this to her husband.

Her husband, the man with the stubbornness of an ox and the protective instincts of a bear. Her husband, who'd been superexcited the week before when she mentioned trying for kid three. Her husband, who would keep a single hair from falling off her head if he could manage it.

Baojia didn't like change. Their plan had always been for Natalie to wait until the kids were in their teens before she turned into an immortal. She was only thirty-eight. She had plenty of time. Another ten years would mean little for an eternity, but missing a year of her children's young lives while she was learning to control vampire instincts felt like a lot.

"Life doesn't always go according to plan." She placed the report on the table and looked at the man who was her doctor, her friend, and soon would be her immortal sire. "He's going to have to see that."

His face was implacable. "Ninety percent survival rate after five years is very good."

"But why?" Natalie leaned forward. "That means a ten percent chance of *not* surviving. Have you thought about it that way?"

His jaw was set. "And if it doesn't look like the treatment will be successful, then we have the conversation then."

"So I'd be risking my immortal health to save my mortal health?"

"If it will give you another five years, yes."

They were in their bedroom and the kids were in bed. Baojia had paced for ten minutes straight before leaning against the door and crossing his arms over his chest in his most stubborn pose. His expression hadn't cracked since they'd walked to Lucien's office at nightfall.

Natalie shook her head. "Why are we fighting over five years?"

"You wanted another baby," he said. "So did I."

"So we have two amazing kids instead of three," she said. "We're already lucky as hell."

"Five years..." He took a deep breath. "Five years gets Sarah to nine. She'll be able to better understand—"

"She already does." Natalie felt tears well in her eyes. "It's not going to be any easier to do it in five years than it would be now. I'll miss things now when I'm healthier or I'll miss things later when I'm possibly still trying to recover from cancer treatment."

He rubbed a hand on his temple. "We shouldn't decide anything right away. We should investigate your options and—"

"Lucien said weeks, not months."

"Dammit, Natalie!" He exploded from the door and came to kneel in front of her. "You don't understand how much this is going to change everything. You won't be able to see your children. Your friends. Your father—"

"I already know that." She put a hand on his cheek and swallowed the lump in her throat. "Don't you think I've thought about it a hundred times just today? And before that?"

His dark eyes pleaded with her. "You won't ever see the sun again. You won't be able to take the kids to the beach. Or go hiking in the redwoods when it's warm."

She whispered, "Don't make this harder than it already is."

He stood. "I'm going to make it harder because I want you to think. I want you to think about everything you're going to give up if you change right now, and I want you to consider traditional medical treatment to give yourself more time." He walked to the door. "I'm going to talk to Makeda. She'll understand."

"Baojia—"

"Let me talk to her." He raised a hand. "I just… I want us to do the best thing. For you and for the family."

He walked out the door, and Natalie put her face in

her hands and cried. She hid in the bathroom and cried into a towel so he wouldn't hear her. She cried until she was wrung out. Then she reached for her phone.

～

"I'D SAY YOU SHOULD ASK FOR A SECOND OPINION," DEZ said. "But it's Lucien. He would have already double- and triple-checked before he said anything."

Natalie tore shreds from the tissue in her hand. "B?"

"Agreed," Beatrice added. "There's no way Lucien would give you a diagnosis unless he was sure."

"So I definitely have cancer." Natalie had her phone on speaker and sat on the floor by the soaking tub in their bathroom. "And Baojia and I already agreed that I was going to turn when the kids were older. So why is he making an issue of this now?"

Both Dez and Beatrice made low muttering noises.

"Men don't like change," Dez said. "Especially when it comes to their wives."

"Unless it's like... sexy new lingerie or something," Beatrice added. "That kind of change is okay."

"That's where I went wrong," Natalie said. "I should have put on a negligee to tell him I had breast cancer."

Beatrice snorted.

Dez said, "Somehow, I think that would have gone worse."

"Ya think?" It was nearly three in the morning, and they'd been talking for an hour. Baojia hadn't come back in the house. Dez was fully awake now, and Beatrice...

Well, Beatrice never slept. She was the absolute best

girlfriend in the world, because if she was in the country —and even if she wasn't—she pretty much always had time to talk you through a crisis.

"Take the kids out of the equation," Dez said. "Why do it now and not wait to try treatment?"

"I can't take the kids out of the equation," Natalie said. "How is that even possible? This has everything to do with the kids."

Beatrice said, "True."

Dez sighed. "Okay, you're right. I can't argue with that."

Both Dez and Beatrice were mothers. Dez's daughter, Carina, was nearly ten, and Beatrice and Giovanni had adopted a toddler the Christmas before. Sadia was two and a half, but Beatrice and Giovanni had quickly adapted to the challenges of parenting her, with lots of help from Dez, Matt, Natalie, and Baojia.

Beatrice said, "At the end of the day, it's your choice. Just like it was mine. Giovanni was pissed at me—"

"You didn't even tell him you were going to do it," Dez said. "I mean, he kind of had a point."

"I'm not saying he didn't, but the fact remains. It's Natalie's decision. She doesn't have to ask for permission," Beatrice said. "Right, Nat?"

"Lucien and Baojia have always had an agreement. And Lucien is fully on board with doing it this way. He doesn't like chemotherapy if I have other options."

"I can see that," Dez said. "And you know you'll have lots of support to help with the kids."

"I'm sure Ariel and Olivia will want to stay around," Natalie said. "But would it be safe?"

"You could come down here," Beatrice said. Both Beatrice and Dez lived in Southern California, where Baojia and Natalie had met.

"Can't. Baojia would be in Ernesto's territory, and even visiting is kind of tricky. Plus, I don't think superconcentrated urban areas are a great idea when you're a newly turned, still-bitey vampire, you know?" She looked around her bathroom. "We're pretty isolated out here."

"Then we can come up there," Beatrice said. "Just know that no matter what, you don't have to do this alone. You will not have to do any of this alone."

The tears came fast and sudden. Natalie clamped a hand over her mouth to keep a sob from coming out.

"Natalie?" Dez asked.

She couldn't speak. She grabbed another tissue and tried to get control of her emotions, but everything seemed to come in a flood.

It's cancer.

Weeks not months.

You won't ever see the sun again. You won't be able to take the kids to the beach. Or go hiking in the redwoods...

You won't have to do this alone.

"Natalie, talk to us," Beatrice said. "Do we need to fly up? I'll get Giovanni to get the plane right now. We can be there in an hour."

"Honey, tell us what's going on," Dez said. "Dammit, I wish I was there."

She just shook her head over and over. It was too much. She didn't want to break down on the phone with her two best friends. She wanted her husband, but he was angry and confused. She wanted her kids, but she didn't want to wake them up. She wanted the world's biggest glass of wine.

She sniffed and blew her nose. "I'm fine."

Two loud groans came from the telephone.

"You're not fucking fine!" Beatrice practically yelled.

Dez said, "That's the most ridiculous thing you've ever said, and I'm counting the time you convinced me to get bangs in grad school."

Beatrice cackled, and Natalie let out a watery laugh. "The bangs weren't that bad."

"They were awful," Beatrice said. "Don't lie."

She couldn't seem to stop the tears. She blew her nose and grabbed another tissue. "I know this is right," she said. "I know this is the right thing to do. I just have to convince him that I know what I'm doing, and I know this is right."

She heard the bedroom door open. She didn't move. She didn't want to talk to her husband, but she also knew she couldn't avoid him. And she had to blow her nose again.

"Natalie"—Beatrice was talking when Baojia opened the bathroom door—"you know what's right for your kids. You're an amazing mom. You and Baojia are amazing parents. You're going to be fine. You will get through this, okay?"

He stared at her, and for the first time, she saw the bare grief in his eyes. The fear. The uncertainty. Natalie held out her arms, and he knelt down and wrapped her in a hard embrace.

"You won't be alone," Dez was saying. "None of you guys have to do this on your own. We're going to figure out the best place to make this happen, and we'll all take turns helping the kids get through this."

Natalie sniffed and Baojia pulled away to get her another Kleenex. He wiped her eyes and pressed kisses to her forehead.

"I'm sorry," he whispered. "I'm sorry, Red."

"It's okay." She hugged his neck and held on for dear life. "This is shit. It's all shit. It wasn't supposed to happen this way."

"Nat?" Dez asked. "George, is that you?"

Baojia managed to crack a smile when Dez used his old nickname. "Hey, Dez. Thanks for being here for Natalie while I was being an idiot."

Natalie sniffed. "Beatrice is on the call too."

"Hey, B."

"Hey." Beatrice sounded sad. "Think about it this way. You have a hell of a lot more options than most families do."

"Yeah." He tucked a piece of Natalie's hair behind her ear. "And I have a sexy-as-hell wife that's gonna be thirty-eight forever. Luckiest man alive."

She traced the only wrinkle he had, a faint line at the corner of his left eye. "Says the guy who looks like he's twenty-nine."

"I've always liked older women."

Natalie snorted and then immediately blew her nose again while Dez and Beatrice laughed.

"Hey, Baojia?" Beatrice said. "I just had an idea. What do you think of everyone getting together for a family Christmas this year?"

His jaw clenched, but Baojia looked into Natalie's eyes. She nodded.

"Yeah." He cleared his throat. "That gives us a few weeks to plan."

"Trust me," Beatrice said. "I know the perfect place for the holidays."

CHAPTER THREE

*N*atalie lounged on the couch of the private jet, drifting in and out of sleep. The sixteen-hour journey from Los Angeles to the remote valley in Chile was nearly halfway over. They'd be stopping in Panama for fuel soon, then another eight hours would take them to Santiago where they'd do a quick stop to take care of paperwork before they continued on to Puerto Montt.

In Natalie's experience, nothing beat international travel with vampires. The few times she and the kids had accompanied Baojia on a work trip, she hadn't had to stand in customs or immigration lines. She rarely had to pay for visas. Was bribery involved? Probably. But when she was traveling with preschoolers, bending her journalistic ethics probably served the greater good.

Beatrice and Giovanni's plane was even more luxurious than the private planes she'd been on before. There was one private stateroom and three narrow compartments added for vampire passengers. The windows were blacked out, and where normal planes had seats, their plane had short couches that could be extended into beds. A television had been installed on one side of the cabin, and four children were gathered around it, watching a cartoon with Beatrice and Giovanni's nanny, Dema.

For the adults, a large library filled one bulkhead. The books were trapped behind clear plastic doors so they wouldn't shuffle during takeoff and landing. There were also games, DVDs, and a video game console. A small kitchen was against the other bulkhead, along with several large storage areas that contained food.

And blood. And blood-wine.

Natalie tried not to shudder. This was going to be her life. Blood would be her primary sustenance. Though she would eat a small amount of human food, she would drink blood, a lot of it during her first year, if she had her facts correct. Just the idea was enough to weird her out.

She loved it when Baojia bit her, so she didn't know why the idea of biting him felt so weird. But it did. It definitely did.

The adults had surrendered the television to the four drowsy children. Baojia, Lucien, Makeda, and Giovanni were all in the vampire sleeping compartments. Beatrice, who never slept, was reading a book behind Dez while Matt and Dez both stretched out on the sleeping couches.

Dez and Matt's daughter, Carina, was the oldest of the kids. She was sitting on the couch with Beatrice's daughter, Sadia, between her legs. Sadia was sucking her thumb and leaning into Carina; the girls were clearly very close. Jake stretched out on the ground in front of the television while Sarah leaned against Dema's side.

Dema rarely spoke, but she kept a close eye on all the

children and smiled a lot, seemingly content to watch her sixth straight animated movie of the trip.

Sarah had already taken a liking to the quiet nanny, which made Natalie regret she couldn't lure Dema away from Giovanni and Beatrice.

Of course, Dema was also a former soldier with medical training who acted as a bodyguard, spoke five languages, and could fly the plane in an emergency. Natalie was pretty sure Jake and Sarah wouldn't need that level of nanny-ing.

She turned in her seat. "Where did you hire Dema?"

Beatrice looked up from her book. "It was a process, but Matt helped, so I'm sure he can consult with you guys if you feel like you need extra help. She was working for a friend of his in Madrid, but she wanted to get back to the West Coast, so it worked out."

"Where is she from?"

"Orange County," Beatrice said. "Her parents are Syrian, so she speaks Syrian Arabic like a native, but she grew up in Anaheim. Language fluency wasn't a requirement for Sadia's nanny, but it was definitely a plus. We wanted her to grow up speaking both Arabic and English fluently and my skills are still developing. Giovanni's are better, but Dema helps a lot."

"Yeah, the plan was for Baojia to only speak Mandarin with the kids and me to only speak English, but we kind of fall down on that. Jake's Mandarin is pretty good, but Sarah's is spotty."

"What do they speak with each other?"

"English," Natalie said. "Unless they're trying to be mean and they think Dad can't hear them. Then it's

Mandarin because they know I only get every other word."

Beatrice laughed. "Kids."

"Tiny hellions," Natalie said quietly. "And we have two. I'm probably going to have to pay double what you do."

Beatrice pursed her lips. "I *highly* doubt that unless you need someone with a pilot's license."

"Good point." She crossed her arms on the back of the seat and rested her chin. "It's so weird. I still feel totally normal. I have a sore spot on my left boob. That's about it."

"The dizzy spells?"

"Once I started getting more sleep, they seemed to go away. Lucien doesn't even think my initial fainting was related to the cancer, but fortunately it forced me to get a physical."

"Who found it? Lucien?"

Natalie shook her head. "Makeda. I love Lucien, but I'm more comfortable with Mak."

Beatrice smiled. "I'm glad she came. I'm looking forward to getting to know her better."

"You'll love her. So will Sadia and Carina. She's great."

"But you're still determined that you want Lucien to…?" Beatrice bared her fangs and made a biting motion.

Natalie couldn't stop the smile. "Yeah. I mean, it would be weird to have Baojia's immortal child sire his wife, wouldn't it?"

Beatrice waved a hand. "Not really. I can think of five or six vampires whose families look like that, actually. Carwyn's daughter is the one who sired his wife, Brigid, though they weren't involved at the time. Immortal families don't look anything like human ones. I mean, Giovanni's son kidnapped and sired my *father*, who eventually sired me." She spread her hands. "Not considered odd by anyone we know."

Natalie shook her head. "Vampires are superweird."

"Aren't we? I know." A shadow crossed Beatrice's face.

"Are you worried about Ben?" Natalie had heard their adopted nephew had changed, but she didn't know the details and she didn't want to pry.

"He's doing okay." Beatrice glanced at Sadia. "He hasn't really called since he went to Mongolia. We just get reports from his sire's assistant. The first few months can be a blur, and you lose track of time a lot, so we're trying not to worry."

Natalie nodded. "Still, I'm sure you'd rather he was with you."

The faint lines around Beatrice's eyes tightened. "He's where he needs to be. Besides, that means you can be in Cochamó. So maybe things worked out exactly like they were supposed to."

Natalie could tell Beatrice was still torn. "Are you and Giovanni sure—"

"The cabin in Cochamó is perfectly set up to keep you and the whole family safe," Beatrice reassured her. "It's where I spent my first year. The cabin is up in the mountains, so I stayed there and Gio went back and forth. Ben stayed at Isabel and Gustavo's house in the valley."

"And he liked it?"

"Are you kidding? It's a cattle ranch with horses and dogs and goats and a million chickens. They go river rafting and rock climbing. Forests everywhere. Ben had his own horse. He ran all over the place; it's kid heaven. Plus Gus still has human family who run the ranch, so there are lots of people to be with the kids during the day."

Natalie smiled. "It sounds great. Jake might never want to leave."

"It was hard getting Ben to leave some years because we'd spend summers down here. And summer for us is their winter! We're headed straight into the nicest time of year."

"I keep forgetting that. We're going to sun! Actual sun."

Beatrice nodded. "Yep, summer for Christmas. The weather is perfect right now."

Her smile felt forced. "Gotta soak up the rays while I can."

Beatrice took a long breath. "Yeah."

"Yeah."

Beatrice got out of her seat, walked around the couch, and sat next to Natalie, putting her arms around her. "It's going to be hard at first. And then it's going to get better. There are lots of isolated places in the mountains for you to go, so you won't feel cooped up. The farmhouse is about two miles away from the cabin, so you'll be far enough away to feel like you won't be a danger. I promise, it's the best place I can think of for your family to be."

"And Carwyn's family—"

"They're amazing." Beatrice glanced at the locked compartments. "Since Lucien is going to sire you, you're going to be an earth vampire, which Carwyn's entire family is. So it's perfect. Seriously, you'll feel so at home you'll probably never want to leave."

Natalie leaned her head on Beatrice's, trying to wrap her mind around being confined to a strange place for a year with no option to leave. "It's going to be fine."

"I promise it will. It might not seem that way all the time, but it's going to be okay." She squeezed Natalie tight. "Remember, you're not alone."

~

Cochamó Valley, Chile

Baojia rode at the back of the party, keeping watch over the children who'd all been rocked to sleep by the movement of the horses as they rode into the valley. The moon filtered through the dense foliage, illuminating the narrow track they were taking through the forest.

Carwyn's son Gustavo had met them at the end of the road—which was literally the end to a road that ran along the coast, over the mouth of a river, and through the mountains until it ended in a dirt track—to lead them into the heart of the isolated refuge in the impenetrable mountain valleys of Patagonia.

The whole party had mounted horses with the children riding along with the adults. Dez and Matt were excited and talking softly while Carina slept in the saddle in front of Matt. It was their first time in the valley, but they'd heard a lot about it over the years.

Lucien and Makeda rode silently next to each other, a tall, regal-looking pair who would be at home in some kind of imperial procession rather than riding workhorses to a cattle ranch. Dema watched them both with undisguised interest.

Beatrice was far more comfortable in the saddle than Baojia had expected. She was riding next to Natalie, who had Jake sitting in front of her.

Giovanni fell back and rode next to Baojia, Sadia sleeping curled up in front of him, not unlike how Sarah was sleeping on Baojia.

"Are you comfortable?" the fire vampire asked.

"I haven't ridden a horse in roughly a hundred years, but I guess it's a little like riding a bike." It probably helped that they were walking slowly through a relatively even section of the forest and the trail followed a river.

"It's not too much farther. Maybe an hour or two."

Giovanni looked at home on a horse, and Baojia was reminded again how old the man was. He'd been alive for over five hundred years. Cars were still new technology.

"What's it like?" Baojia asked. "To be able to move around the world so quickly now? Yesterday we were in Los Angeles."

"It's astonishing." He smoothed a hand down Sadia's back, and the little girl sighed deeply. "She'll never know a world where the entirety of the globe isn't a few days' journey away. Astonishing."

Baojia thought of the weeks he'd spent crossing the Pacific Ocean in a steamship, crowded into accommodations far less comfortable than a private jet. "It is astonishing."

"In some ways it's made everything far simpler."

"And far more complicated in others," Baojia said.

"Yes."

Baojia debated asking the question, but he was rabidly curious. "Can I ask you about Ben?"

Giovanni's eyes flicked to Lucien. "It's complicated."

"Family usually is." Baojia had only heard rumors, but he knew Giovanni was right. "He'll be all right. Most of my own security staff aren't as tough as your nephew."

Giovanni glanced at Sadia. "She's going to miss him. Ben is one of her favorites. They usually talk on the computer once a week. So far we've been able to distract her, but she's beginning to ask more often."

The Italian didn't say what he was probably thinking: far harder to distract two growing and curious children from missing their own mother.

Baojia glanced at his daughter. Sarah was an even mix of Natalie and Baojia, unlike Jake, who was a small carbon copy of his father. Her dark hair curled slightly, like Natalie's did. Sarah's skin was fair, and she had freckles across her nose. Her eyes were brown like his, but her chin and nose were the exact shape of his wife's.

He knew other vampires wondered how he and Natalie had conceived children who so obviously resembled both biological parents when natural conception was impossible.

Other vampires could mind their own business.

Sarah began to slump to one side, and Baojia nudged her back into place. "She'll enjoy all these trees when she's awake, though I may have to lock her up during the day to keep her from breaking all her limbs. She wants to climb *everything*."

Giovanni looked at Sarah, then at Sadia. "Does the complete and abject terror ever go away?"

Baojia looked up. "You tell me. How old is Caspar now?"

Giovanni smiled sadly. "I know it sounds odd, but I didn't worry the same way about Caspar when he was small. He was a Jewish child living in England during World War II. The terror of German bombs and Nazi invasion seemed far more pressing than the terror of climbing trees or childhood illness."

"That doesn't sound odd." Baojia hadn't known any of that about Caspar's background. He'd only known that Giovanni had adopted Caspar when he was a boy and raised him overseas. "That sounds practical. You have to prioritize threats."

Giovanni mused, "Caspar was such a survivor—it didn't even occur to me that he wouldn't make it to adulthood. Isn't that strange?"

"She's a survivor too." Baojia nodded at Sadia. "And she has a large family now who will do anything to keep her safe. And a nanny trained in krav maga."

Giovanni smiled. "Is it that obvious?"

"There's an efficiency about the way she moves," Baojia said. "I've seen it most in professionals trained in krav maga. It was a guess."

"A good one."

"Guessing is my job," Baojia said. "We only call it threat assessment because it looks better on business cards. But to answer your question"—Baojia glanced down at Sarah —"no. In my experience, the terror never leaves you. Small humans are remarkably fragile. It's amazing they're even born, isn't it?" He brushed a lock of Sarah's hair from her eyes. "An everyday miracle. Every night they get a little sturdier. A little stronger." His eyes moved to Jake. "But even then—even when they're grown like Ben—we will always worry. And with good reason. We know the worst of what this world can be."

"We do." Giovanni's face was stoic. "I try to remember the best it can be to keep myself sane."

CHAPTER FOUR

*B*eatrice felt the energy of familiar ground in her blood. Though she wasn't an earth vampire, every rock and stream of the valley felt familiar. The crystal-clear night sky soothed her eyes, and the smell of the wind settled her heart.

Home.

She'd been returning to this place every year for as long as she'd known Giovanni Vecchio. She came here to heal. She came here to grieve. She came to find joy in stolen moments of peace and a pure river that quenched her soul. Waterfalls that dotted the slopes of the mountains and a winding river that cut through the valley.

Cochamó was home. And now she got to share it with the people who had become her chosen family. She hadn't been painting a rosy picture for Natalie because of her circumstances. There was no better place to make the transition to immortal life.

As they broke through the trees and into the clearing

that marked the boundaries of the grazing land, Giovanni rode up beside her and reached for her hand. She squeezed it, knowing he was thinking the same thing she was.

"I wanted it to be here for him."

"I know."

Even thinking of Ben made her heart hurt. "Do Isabel and Gustavo know?"

"I'm sure Carwyn told them."

"Are he and Brigid here yet?"

"They are. Carwyn has been helping Carla with something, and I'm not sure what it is. But he's been in Peru for a while. I think Brigid just joined him."

"Peru?"

"Or Bolivia?" Giovanni shrugged. "I'm honestly not sure."

Carwyn's daughter Carla was Gus's twin sister, and the only one of Carwyn's living children Beatrice had never met. She was notoriously reclusive and didn't often leave the wilderness.

"Is Carla in Cochamó?"

Giovanni shook his head. "I don't think so."

Beatrice saw lights in the distance and the red-gold flicker of a campfire. As they approached, a shout went up, and soon after the sound of horses galloping drew toward them.

Sadia woke from her perch in Giovanni's arms and looked around. "Baba?"

"Yes, Sadia?"

"We home?" She yawned.

"We are in the adventure place," Giovanni said. "Remember?"

"Mmm." She pressed her face into Giovanni's chest. "Ben?"

"No, Sadia. Ben isn't here this time."

Beatrice listened to their quiet conversation. Sadia still didn't speak as much as other children, but Beatrice was beginning to think that was just her personality. She spoke when she wanted to, but she was an observer by nature.

Giovanni was endlessly patient. When Beatrice became overwhelmed, frustrated, or worried, he was a well of calm. He never called Sadia by anything but her name. There were no nicknames like the teasing "princesa" that Isadora and Beatrice used for the little girl when she was being obstinate. Giovanni called their daughter Sadia, and in his mouth their child's name sounded like a blessing.

Four horses from the ranch drew close, and Beatrice saw who rode them. Carwyn was at the front, his red hair flying up in the wind. He wore a colorful wrap around his shoulders and a grin on his face. When he reached the party, he went directly to Natalie.

"There you are." He reached across and enveloped her in a wild embrace. "I'm so glad you came to us." He sat back and put his hand on her cheek. "What a clever woman you are."

Jake was sitting upright, blinking his eyes. "Mom?"

"Jakey, this is our friend Carwyn. This house belongs to his family."

The boy took a deep breath and yawned. "V-vampire?"

"Indeed I am." Carwyn stuck his hand out to Baojia. "Good to see you, my friend. It has been too long."

"Thank you," Baojia said solemnly. "I will never be able to repay you for welcoming us like this."

"These aren't debts we keep track of, are they?" Carwyn's smile never wavered. "Not between friends."

As they drew closer to the ranch, Gus began barking orders to the others on horseback, directing them to the packhorses and those carrying luggage. The party rode past the first set of corrals filled with cattle that had been penned for the night, and within a few minutes, all the children and humans were wide awake as they rode into the compound. Dogs barked, horses stamped, and cattle lowed in the background.

"Dad!" Jake sat up and pointed. "Look at all the dogs!"

"I see them." Baojia muttered something under his breath.

Sarah sat up and looked around. "What's that smell?"

"Cows," Carwyn said. "Do you like hamburger?"

"Oh." Sarah's eyes went wide. "Are these hamburger cows?"

Some of the adults laughed, but Jake looked at his sister disdainfully. "All cows are hamburger cows."

"No, they're not!" Sarah looked indignant. "Henrietta is a milk cow."

"An excellent point, Miss Sarah. We have milk cows here as well," Carwyn said. "I'm not sure if any of them are named Henrietta."

Beatrice recognized the name of a familiar children's storybook cow and hoped that Sarah's bovine love wouldn't be too sorely tested by spending a year on a working cattle ranch.

Carina pointed. "Mom! Mom, they have little goats. Look!"

"I see that."

Sadia said nothing. She was wide-eyed and silent as she took everything in.

As they entered the ranch yard, Beatrice scented the aroma of meat cooking on a grill. They passed the last set of corrals and rode the horses between the houses and toward the long red barn behind the bunkhouses.

Friendly hands waved from the porch, human and vampire intermingling. In Gus and Isabel's valley refuge, there were no secrets and all the humans were accustomed to the immortals. For the most part, those who occupied the ranch were family of one sort or another. The few others were trusted friends and employees.

Beatrice rode up to the barn and dismounted, tying her horse's reins to a long hitching post before she turned and held her hands up to Giovanni. He handed their daughter down, and Beatrice wrapped Sadia's arms around her neck.

"How is my *princesa*?" Beatrice asked. *"Cómo estás? Estás cansada?"*

Sadia spoke enough Spanish to shake her head. No, she wasn't sleepy, though her eyes said otherwise. Beatrice pulled her wrap close around Sadia and pressed her cheek to hers. "Are you cold?"

She nodded.

"Let's go wait by the fire, okay?" Beatrice looked around for Dema, but she was helping Natalie and Baojia with their two kids. Giovanni dismounted and passed the reins to one of Gus's ranch hands before he took Beatrice's hand and walked back toward the fire.

At the back of the yard was Gustavo and Isabel's large ranch house with all the main rooms of the compound, the dining hall, library, and large living rooms. Jutting off the side was a simple chapel with a cross rising from the top. Fronting the house was a deep porch that provided shade and rain protection year-round.

Bordering the open yard on the far side of the house were various outbuildings. Bunkhouses, storage rooms, and offices ran down one side. Mudrooms, bathrooms, and a large ranch kitchen bordered the other. The two branches of the house reached out to the yard and the narrow valley, as if embracing it.

Beatrice saw smoke rising around the compound from various wood-burning stoves inside the dwellings, and the large bonfire in the middle of the yard was surrounded by chairs and log benches where all the guests and their hosts were beginning to gather.

They sat, and a tray of steaming mugs came around. Tea for the adults and cocoa for the children. The air was cold enough that their breath steamed in the night, though Beatrice knew it would be dramatically warmer for the humans during the day.

Isabel, Carwyn's daughter and owner of the ranch, stood up once everyone had gathered around. "Welcome to all our guests. We're so glad you were able to make it to the valley for Christmas this year. Though we don't have snow, we do have lots of Christmas trees!" She smiled and a few people laughed. "I hope the children are excited about decorating them."

Carina was nearly bouncing in her seat. "I like decorating trees."

"Excellent."

In short order, everyone was sorted into rooms and cabins. Beatrice and Giovanni's cabin was up in the foothills above the valley, miles from the main ranch, so until Natalie and Baojia needed it, their whole party would remain in the valley, occupying rooms in the guest wing of the house and the many small, wood-shingled cabins scattered around the ranch. All were fitted with locks and shutters so they were vampire-safe, and they were within walking distance of the ranch house and kitchen.

Giovanni put his arm around Beatrice and kissed the top of Sadia's head. "This is going to be the strangest summer camp ever."

Brigid Connor, fire vampire, security specialist for Patrick Murphy of Dublin and wife of Carwyn ap Bryn nearly ran into her bedroom at the ranch and locked the door behind her, leaning against it and heaving a long sigh of relief.

Carwyn looked up from the book he was reading on the bed. "Done socializing, are we?"

"Jaysus, there's so many people here." Brigid shook her head. She walked to the bed and crawled across it so her husband could pet her. "I'm sure every last one of them is a fecking delight on their own, but the lot of them all at once…"

"More than a bit overwhelming." Carwyn ran his fingers through Brigid's pixie-cut hair. "Even for me. And I like people."

"I like people," Brigid protested. "In small groups. Even in medium groups. But that was a herd, my fine man."

Carwyn smiled and scooped her up and into his arms,

depositing Brigid on his lap so he could snuggle her properly. She'd been on the continent, seeing to a few things for Murphy before she caught a boat to join him in Cochamó for the Christmas holiday, so he was making up for lost time.

He caught her mouth in a kiss. Then another one. Soon enough, he was stealthily inching his hand up her shirt.

"You know," she murmured against his lips. "I can take everything off if that's what you're aiming for."

"But it's so much more fun when I feel like we're sneaking around."

Brigid smiled and tilted her head to the side to allow Carwyn to nibble her neck. He was a man who thrived on affection, so separations were never ideal. The side benefit was feeling adored when they were reunited.

"You know," Brigid said as the nibbles turned to long, laving kisses, "I was down there, looking at all those couples with young children and thinking—"

Carwyn's head popped up. "What? You were thinking of what?" His eyes were wide, and he looked slightly terrified.

Brigid began to laugh. "Calm down, Father. I was just thinking that I was relieved we hadn't adopted any little ones of our own. They're nice to visit, but feck, they're so much work."

"Oh, thank the Lord." Carwyn leaned his forehead against her shoulder. "You gave me a fright."

"I was half-afraid you were going to be enthusiastic about the idea." Brigid shifted her legs so she could straddle his lap.

Carwyn took her mouth again. "I just have"—kisses on

41

her mouth and across her cheek—"so many children"—his hands inching up her sides, teasing her skin with delicious, tingling amnis—"already."

Brigid sank into his kiss and rested her arms on his massive shoulders. When she was in a teasing mood, she called him *carnín*. Her little mountain. It was a ridiculous nickname, so of course her husband loved it.

"Never fear," Brigid said. "I don't want any babies, thank you very much." She rocked her hips into Carwyn's, enjoying the rise of the other mountain in the room. "I am not in favor of sharing you any more than I already do."

"I'm yours." He flipped her over and settled between her legs. "Completely. Snap your fingers and I'm there, darling girl."

She began unbuttoning his pants. "Snap my fingers?"

He reached down and slid a hand down the back of her pants. "Unless you'd rather do something else with them."

Brigid grinned and reached into his pants. "I think I have a few ideas."

Carwyn groaned and pressed his face into her neck. "Please." His fangs slid along the side of her throat, and his tongue flicked against her pulse. "Please demonstrate."

"If you insist."

CHAPTER FIVE

"Know what I'm really pissed about?" Natalie was sitting on the edge of the river, watching as the four California kids splashed on the edges.

Dema was holding Sadia's hand while she waded, and Natalie was keeping a close eye on Sarah, who wasn't allowed go past the big rocks.

Jake and Carina were both excellent swimmers and the water wasn't moving fast, so Natalie and Dez were sitting in the sun, enjoying the afternoon warmth.

Dez said, "The obvious answer would be that you're pissed about getting breast cancer, so I know it's not that."

Natalie put a hand on her startlingly pale white legs. "Cellulite for eternity. I know it's superficial, but I'm going to have bumpy thighs and stretch marks for possibly hundreds of years."

Dez started to laugh.

"I mean," Natalie continued, "I thought I had more

time. I was going to lose ten pounds or so. Trim up. Definitely get better arms, you know?"

"I remember your talking about Michelle arms."

"Yes! Right? But nope. No time. I'm stuck for all eternity with preschool-mom bod."

"What did you think you were going to do about the cellulite?" Dez stretched her own legs out. "I mean, everyone has some. Beatrice probably does, and she changed ten years ago."

"I don't know." Natalie started to laugh. "Isn't there laser surgery or something? Celebrity vampires probably don't have cellulite."

Dez dropped her voice. "Are there celebrity vampires? Is that a thing?"

"I don't think so, but the point remains. There is probably some medical way of getting rid of all these bumps, but I'm never going to find it because I have breast cancer." She shook her head. "Fucking breast cancer."

"It really bites."

They repeated the common refrain together. "And not in a sexy vampire way."

"Exactly," Natalie said. "Not at all in a sexy vampire way." A wave of exhaustion started to creep up on her. "Dez, can you watch mine?"

"No problem." Dez reached over and tilted Natalie's hat over her eyes. "Lie down and nap if you want to. I'll throw a towel over you if you start to burn."

"Thanks." The grass on the riverbank was soft and long, mingling with sand and small pebbles. They'd been at the ranch for three days, and every afternoon they'd spent with the kids outside. Natalie was determined to soak up as much sun as she could. Christmas was four days away, which meant she had less than a week left of being human.

She still hadn't wrapped her mind around it. She wasn't excited. She wasn't dreading it. It was as if an appointment she'd made years before was finally rolling around. Or company showing up unexpectedly. It wasn't bad, but you'd forgotten to make a big enough dinner and all the nice dishes were dirty.

There were so many things she'd been meaning to do, and she hadn't because… she was busy!

She'd been busy teaching Jake how to ride a bike and making sure Sarah ate green things.

She'd been balancing work and the kids' school stuff.

She'd been trying to figure out if Jake having a dog was feasible or would cause a whole new set of problems.

She'd been trying to find gymnastics lessons for Sarah that didn't involve driving sixty miles both ways.

And she'd been trying to remember to kiss her husband more often because she'd realized a couple of months before that she'd gone three days without kissing Baojia, and that was simply unacceptable when you were married to a man that hot.

Nothing in her life was simple. Every problem solved seemed to create two new issues, and now…

And now.

Her life had boiled down to the barest essentials.

There was no school. No work. No plans.

There were only the people she loved who had come around her, and the precious hours of human life slipping away. If being sick weren't forcing her to sleep every day, she'd skip sleep altogether. Another hour gone. Another minute ticked by.

Her eyes were closed, and the sun warmed her cheeks. She could feel Dez playing with her hair, braiding the ends, spreading the warm red across the grass.

Natalie's eyes fluttered open. "How long?"

Dez looked at her watch. "Maybe twenty minutes?"

Twenty minutes of sunlight gone.

"What do you want to do?" Dez asked. "We're deciding cellulite is sexy and desirable, so let's focus on what you want to do before... you know."

"Before Lucien drains my blood and makes me drink his and I turn into a ferocious creature of the night?"

Dez patted her head. "It's so cute how you think you're going to be ferocious."

"I *am* going to be ferocious." Natalie snapped her teeth. "For real, I'll be totally ferocious. A complete badass."

"Right." Dez muttered, "At least we won't have to worry about you running into traffic anymore."

"I only did that because Councilman Vargas was dodging the question! He's the one who crossed the street. I just followed him."

"Into traffic, Natalie!"

She shrugged. "No one hit me. I knew what I was doing. And if that damn cameraman hadn't been there for channel 2o, none of you would have even known it happened."

"But he was, and we did."

She wouldn't be able to work like she had before. You couldn't be an investigative reporter for a major newspaper if you couldn't go anywhere during the day.

"What do I want to do?" She had to distract herself. "Other than lose that ten pounds?"

"I mean..." Dez got out her phone. "I can try to find

some Wi-Fi and look online to see what part of your body you can cut off if you want to streamline, but yeah, I'm thinking other than weight loss. One, it's super not important, and your ass is already enviable. Also, probably not feasible in a week. What *important things* do you want to do before you turn into a vampire?"

Natalie sat up. "Like… a bucket list?"

"Kinda. You're not dying. That's the point. But your human body is *kinda* dying? So yeah. Kind of a Nat-being-human bucket list."

Natalie watched the kids playing in the river. "Spend time in the sun with the kids as much as possible."

"Done. Good one." Dez got out the small notebook she always kept in her purse. "Okay, what else?"

"Are you writing this down?"

"Yes." She scribbled something and held it out so Natalie could see. On the paper, she'd written: Nat's Super-Awesome and Amazing Bucket O' Blood List.

Natalie laughed. "I like the little vampire flourish there."

Dez waved her hand. "Come on. What else, future badass?"

"Uh…" She took a deep breath. "What can vampires not do?"

"Sun is the obvious one."

"Oh!" Natalie's eyes lit up. "I want a tattoo!"

"Oh, good one." Dez wrote it down. "Plus if you get it now, it'll never fade or anything, right?"

"I'll have to check on that, but probably not."

"What else?"

"Mmmm. Kind of goes with playing outside, but get as tan as possible without turning into a lobster."

Dez nodded as she wrote. "Always a fine, fine line with our pale Irish skin, but we'll do our best."

"Do you really think weight lifting to get Michelle arms is out of the question?"

"How important are biceps to you really?"

"Good point." Natalie narrowed her eyes. "What won't I be able to— Oooh! I need to get drunk."

Dez winced. "Are you sure?"

"Load up on aspirin and don't talk to me about sulfites, you ninny. We're getting smashed. At least one night."

"All right." Dez groaned a little writing that one down. "What else?"

"Rock climbing!"

"You do realize you're going to turn into an earth vampire, right?"

"Exactly. Once I'm a vampire, there won't be any challenge in rock climbing. I want to try it when I can still get an adrenaline rush."

"Okay, fair enough." Dez wrote it down.

"Watch the sunrise every morning."

"Definitely. And the sunset."

Natalie smiled. "I do that already. That's when Baojia wakes up."

"Aww." Dez put her pencil down. "You'll never have to say goodbye, Nat. Have you thought about that? You'll never have to say goodbye."

"Nope." Natalie felt her heart swell. "That's the best part."

"More." Dez picked up her pen again.

"Waterskiing?"

"We can try."

"Kayaking?"

"Definitely. I saw some kayaks in the barn."

"Scuba diving?"

Dez pursed her lips. "But wouldn't diving actually be better after you turn, because then you don't have to wear any of that awful gear 'cause you won't need to breathe?"

"Good point. Leave scuba diving off."

"Okay, what else?"

"Lots and lots of food!"

Dez glanced over her shoulder. "With these hosts, I don't see that being a problem."

"Oh." Natalie clapped her hands. "I know what I want. Like, really want. Thanksgiving dinner."

Dez frowned. "But we just had Thanksgiving."

"And I was grumpy and feeling nauseous and over-worked," Natalie said. "This time, I'm going to know it's my last one as a human. I'll be able to stuff myself with pie. Be able to eat a bunch of turkey and fall asleep on the couch."

"I get you." Dez started writing. "We may be limited on food, but I'll talk to Isabel. I'm sure we can figure out something." She flipped the list over and showed Natalie. "Okay, this is your bucket list?"

Natalie nodded.

"Then we'd better get to work."

~

BAOJIA LOOKED AT THE LIST NATALIE HAD COPIED FROM Dez's notebook. "Mountain climbing? Waterskiing?" He looked up with a frown. "You've never done either of those things."

49

Leave it to Baojia to focus on the details. "I know, but I always meant to."

He was still reading the list. "Oh, come on. A *tattoo*?"

"I never got one, but I always wanted one, and I think once I'm immortal, it'll be kind of impossible, right?"

"I think your body would just push the ink out," he muttered. "What the hell kind of tattoo do you want?" He lifted his head. "What am I saying? We're in the middle of nowhere. You're not going to find a tattoo place anywhere close."

Her eyes lit up. "Gus said there's a guy in the nearest town by the mouth of the river—he does them in his kitchen."

His expression didn't evoke confidence. "You want a guy who does tattoos in his *kitchen* to put something on your body that you're going to have for eternity?"

"He might be really good!"

Baojia sat on the edge of the bed and stared at her list. "I've had over a hundred years of life. It's been good. You killing me now would be fine except that we have two young children to take care of."

She sat next to him and rubbed his shoulder. "It's just a tattoo."

"I'm not worried about the tattoo. I'm worried about the rock climbing. And the waterskiing—"

"I think we can take the waterskiing off—"

"Oh, *can we?*" He stood. "Natalie, this is… ridiculous."

Oh no he didn't. "Excuse me?"

"You have *cancer*. Your body is already fighting to stay well right now. And you want to…" He shook the paper in his hand. "Seriously?"

She rose to her feet. "Do you really think I'm so stupid

that I'm going to risk my life? You think I'm gonna get sicker in the next week? Do you think I don't feel what's happening in my own body?" She pointed a finger at him. "Why do you always do this? Do you want me to just curl up and hide for the next week?"

"I want you to stay alive!"

"I'm *going* to stay alive." She snatched the list from his hand. "You're getting everything you wanted. You get me with you forever, in a bulletproof, fall-proof, car-proof body—"

"Not fair," he growled.

"With *cellulite*!" She waved the list in his face. "So I get to have my list."

"Why are you talking about cellulite?" He put his hands on his hips, his eyes steely. "Just *please* do not go mountain climbing."

"Shove it." She walked out the door and was relieved when he didn't follow her.

They were staying in the guest wing of the main house, Natalie and Baojia in one room, Sarah and Jake in the connecting room. It would be their room for the next year.

Well, not *her* room. Her room was going to be in an isolated cabin in the middle of nowhere where she couldn't see any of her human friends or family because she could easily lose control and kill them.

So that sounded fun.

Natalie turned the corner and nearly ran into Brigid Connor, Carwyn's wife, who was wearing a leather jacket, black shoulder holsters, and ripped-up jeans.

Yes. Perfect person.

"Hi!" Natalie said.

"Hello." Brigid smiled politely.

"Want to get a horse and ride into town so I can get a tattoo from a guy who tattoos people in his kitchen?"

Brigid stared at her for a long time. "Feck yeah, that sounds like savage craic."

"I don't know what that means, but you should definitely come along."

"Well done." She put her hand on Natalie's shoulder. "Let's get the girls."

CHAPTER SIX

*B*aojia burst into the living room. "Where are they?"

Lucien looked up from the book he was reading by the fire. "If you're referring to our wives and partners, I believe they have all ridden into town to accompany your wife on her tattoo adventure."

He shook his head. This was what he got for being the responsible one who put the children to bed. Granted, it was his turn, but leave it to Natalie to take advantage of his absence to do something ridiculous.

"Did you not want her to get one?" Carwyn looked over his shoulder. The children had decorated the Christmas tree just after sundown, but since they were all short, the upper level of the tree was more than a little naked. "I'd get one if I could. Wish it had been traditional when I was human."

Carwyn was redistributing ornaments from the lower three feet of the tree to the higher branches while Lucian and Giovanni read. Matt was browsing a picture album on the coffee table. Baojia walked over and helped Carwyn with the tree. "She's just… impulsive. God knows what she's going to get."

"It's her body," Giovanni said. "She's the one who'll have to live with it."

"Unless she gets it someplace she can't see and he can." Carwyn grinned. "That'd be an excellent joke."

"I really don't agree," Baojia muttered.

Giovanni put down his book. "I have a feeling that Baojia is having a harder time with the idea of change than the actual tattoo."

He turned and looked at the collection of men around him. Giovanni looking superior. Carwyn looking up for anything. Matt, who appeared amused. And Lucien, an island of calm and reason.

Baojia turned to Lucien. "She's facing enormous changes, and I don't think she realizes how much this is going to alter her life."

"Of course not," he said. "How could she possibly understand that?"

"But she has flatly refused to seek human treatment for the cancer."

Matt cleared his throat. "Baojia, why would she?"

Carwyn walked around the tree and stood next to Baojia. The large man was an affectionate person, but he didn't touch Baojia, which he appreciated.

"It was always going to happen," Carwyn said. "You'd both planned on it."

"Not this soon," he said quietly. "Not when the children—"

"They'll miss her," Giovanni said. "But in the long run,

her changing now might be easier than when they're older."

"How?" Baojia was trying not to lose his temper. "How will it possibly be easier?" All these men save for Matt had experienced exactly or nearly exactly what he was experiencing now—the transition of their wives or partners from human to immortal. "How is it easier now when the children are so young?"

"Teenagers are complicated," Giovanni said. "They get to a certain age and they think they're allowed to have an opinion on everything."

A low grumble of agreement around the room.

Matt said, "It's already starting with Carina, and she's not even ten."

"Really?" Baojia said.

Carwyn looked at Giovanni. "Do you remember Caspar at that age?"

Giovanni muttered something that sounded like a curse in Italian. "If I could have legally sent that boy away from the age of fourteen to twenty, I would have done it."

"That's surprising," Baojia said.

"Not really." Gustavo entered the room. "You're talking about teenagers?"

"Yes."

"Counting nieces, nephews, and all the ones that came after, I've had twenty-seven on the ranch."

Giovanni winced.

"Trust me," Gus said. "If there are any big family changes, it's better to do them when the children are young. Much easier to distract. You and Natalie are doing the right thing."

"I am so glad I don't have any children," Lucien said quietly.

"I was just thinking the same thing," Carwyn said.

"Hey!" Gus look at Carwyn with a grin. "What am I? Chopped liver?"

"I got you when you were a grown man," Carwyn said. "I find that's the ideal time to adopt children."

Baojia felt some of his nerves settle, but it was still hard to see a bright side through the tangle of the unknown. He'd been with Natalie for eight years. He knew who human Natalie was. He had studied her. He had made himself an expert.

He knew what made her happy and what made her sad. He knew what sounds she loved and what scents she hated. He knew what food she craved and what drinks made her tipsy. He knew exactly where to touch her when he wanted to make her gasp.

The Natalie that was coming, he knew nothing about. What would she be? Who would she be? Would she be as caring a mother? As nurturing? Would she see him in the same light?

Would she love him? Would she love their family?

He sat next to Lucien and stared at the fire in the stone hearth. "Change is difficult."

"But it's necessary." He put a hand on Baojia's shoulder. "I have faith in both of you. You will make it through this. And when you do, you will find a connection that is even more than what you have now. A connection that is eternal."

He nodded. What could he do? Nothing. The only thing that was sure to cure his wife was immortality. And the only thing more frightening than Natalie changing was a world where she didn't exist.

DEZ EYED THE NEEDLE WITH TREPIDATION. "SHOULD I?"

Beatrice, Brigid, and Natalie all cheered her on. "Yes!"

"Absolutely."

"Do it. Do it. Do it." The chant was from Natalie.

Dez was sitting in the kitchen of the small house in the countryside, staring at the beautiful work on Natalie's shoulder. "It's really beautiful."

The man working in the small kitchen in the modest house was a true artist. He'd shown them page after page of photographs in several albums that convinced Natalie she was putting her eternal skin into good hands. She'd chosen something simple, and she loved it.

Now Dez was feeling the urge.

She turned to Makeda, the only person in the room who wasn't cheering her on. "What do you think?"

Makeda looked thoughtful. "I don't think I know you well enough to have an opinion."

"That means you're the perfect person to be objective."

Beatrice pointed at Makeda. "That's an excellent point."

Natalie eased her shirt over her shoulder and turned to Dez. "If you found something you love, then you should do it. It doesn't hurt that much."

Which was a lie. It hurt like hell, but Natalie wasn't going to tell Dez that, or she'd wimp out.

Beatrice chanted. "Do it. Do it. Do it."

"Come on," Brigid said. "Don't be a ninny."

"I don't know you well," Makeda said. "But I will say that one of my sisters has two tattoos. She got them several years ago, and she still loves both of them."

"What are they?"

"Birds. She's an avian biologist."

"Interesting," Beatrice said. "I'm filing that away."

The poor tattoo artist looked tired.

Natalie asked, "Do you have time tonight? We can always come back another night. It's late."

The man asked, "You have cash?"

"Yep," Dez said.

He shrugged. "Then I have time. I'll make coffee."

He was unfazed by the late hour. It was nearly two in the morning, and it had taken about two hours to get from the ranch into town. Natalie caught Brigid checking the time regularly, making sure they didn't cut it too close.

"Do you like this?" Makeda pointed to a photograph of a poppy.

"If he can make it orange, like a California poppy, it'd be perfect." The poppy in the photograph was red.

The artist asked, "Can someone show me a picture?"

Natalie got her phone out and looked for a picture she'd taken last spring of the poppies. She showed it to the artist, who nodded and started to make up a sketch.

"No problem," he said. "I can make it that color."

"Tattoo is a go!" Beatrice said. "Yes!"

Brigid, who'd been hanging out by the door, said, "Going to get more drinks. What'll ya have?"

"Beer."

"Gin and something."

"Whiskey."

"Water."

Brigid cocked her head at Makeda. "Water?"

Makeda asked, "What's wrong with water?"

"Because we're out with the girls," Brigid said. "That's what's wrong with water. I'll get you a whiskey."

"That's really okay."

"Whiskey!" She looked at the tattoo artist. "Beer?"

The man nodded. "Beer."

"I'll be back." She turned, then spun back. "You"—she pointed at Makeda—"come with me. I'll need the extra hands."

Makeda rose from her chair. "I am more than happy to help."

The small town at the edge of the water was the gateway to the many national parks in the region as well as being a hub for ranchers and farmers who needed to trade. The town consisted of a clutch of houses, a church, a school, a general store with lots of camping equipment, and two different pubs. One of the pubs was called Gato Negro, the Black Cat, and the other was simply called Irish Pub, which amused Brigid to no end.

Natalie, Beatrice, and Dez waited while the artist applied the stencil to Dez's ankle. Within few moments, the tattoo needle had buzzed on and the artist had started the outline.

"Oh, you bitch!" Dez spit out. "This hurts like a mother."

Natalie tried not to cackle. "It'll be fine. I wonder if it hurts worse on the ankle?"

"I bet it does," Beatrice said.

"Uh-huh."

"You are both lying liars who lie." Dez closed her eyes and hummed loudly. "Where's my beer?"

Over the next hour, the artist carefully outlined the small flower before he filled it in with vivid golden orange and began shading it. Green and orange were brilliant against Dez's pale skin while the black and grey of Natalie's new ink complemented her freckles.

"You know," Brigid said, peeking at Natalie's ink again. "I'm quite happy you're..." She glanced at the artist. "...taking the path you are. Not enough of our kind with freckles. Even in Ireland."

Natalie's eyes went wide. "You don't think..."

"What?"

"Do they fade? Do you think it's like... a side effect?"

Brigid wrinkled her nose. "Oh, that'd be horrible, wouldn't it? But no! My fine man has plenty of freckles, just not on his nose like you. So they mustn't fade."

That was a relief. Natalie had hated her freckles as a child, but she'd grown to love them, especially after Sarah was born. Baojia called them her personal constellations. Speaking of constellations...

"Are the skies clearing up?" Natalie asked.

"Yes," Makeda said, finishing her second beer. She'd drunk the whiskey and asked for another, but then switched to beer when the pub had closed down. "I can see the stars. And the Southern Cross! That's lovely."

The artist was finishing up Dez's tattoo, Brigid had stocked up on beers for the ride home, but the night was getting shorter and shorter. The skies had threatened rain on the way into town, but the women had soldiered on, unwilling to let a little rain get in the way of their girls' night out. Natalie was relieved to know they wouldn't get rained on as they made their way back to the valley once the tattoos were done.

"Do you think we'll be able to do this again?" Natalie asked.

"Tell you what," Brigid said. "I will commit to a year from now, dragging my reluctant arse onto a giant ship—because you know I hate sea travel—and making my way down here to do this again." She lifted her beer. "Though maybe without the tattoos. Is everyone in?"

"I am in," Makeda said. "Also, Lucien will be here for the full year, so I'll likely be in the area as often as possible."

Natalie's mouth fell open. "Really? He's planning on the whole year?"

Makeda cocked her head. "Of course. He wouldn't dream of leaving you."

"But Baojia—"

"It's not…" Makeda glanced at the artist. "It's not the same. You'll need both of them. I would have been lost without Kato, and even with him, I still missed Baojia terribly. Plus I want to be there for Sarah and Jake. I'll have to go back to California periodically, but as long as I can manage, I'll be here with you."

Natalie's buzz was turning melancholy just as the artist was wrapping up Dez's poppy.

"I love you guys so much." She sniffed and took another long drink of beer. "I just can't imagine doing this alone."

Beatrice took care of paying the tattoo artist while the rest of them made their way out to the street and to one of the many hitching posts in town. Since roads were hit and miss, they weren't the only people riding. Though they'd seen quad bikes a few places, horses seemed to be far more popular with the locals.

They mounted up—Dez needing the most help between the new tattoo and half a dozen beers—and headed back toward the end of the road and the forest path that would lead them back to the ranch.

Natalie was starting to get more and more comfortable on the horse. She nudged her mare up to Beatrice and bumped her shoulder. "Howdy, partner."

"Howdy yourself." Beatrice grinned. "How you feeling?"

"I am going to have the queen bitch of headaches tomorrow, and I don't even care."

Beatrice laughed. "Good. Make sure you take aspirin before you go to bed."

"Baojia is pissed at me," Natalie said. "And I don't get why. I mean… he wanted this. For years he's worried about me every"—she let out a little burp—"every time I even left the house, you know? I would have done it years ago, but he wanted to wait. And now… Do you think he doesn't really want to be with me forever? I mean… that's a really lucking… fong time. You know what I mean."

Beatrice put a hand on her shoulder to steady her. "Don't even think that way. He's just not a man who likes change. You know this."

"I changed the comforter on the bed last spring," Natalie said. "We'd had the same damn blanket on the bed for like five years. It was all stained. So I got this really pretty one, and you know what he said?"

"He wanted the old one back?"

"Yes!" She shook her head and immediately regretted it. "Wow. There are a lot of lights in the forest now."

"Nope. Still just the one path with solar lamps."

"Really?" Natalie squinted. "Nooooo. There's more."

Beatrice was laughing again. "To sum up, Baojia is a totally normal vampire who doesn't like change. He's probably worried you're feeling pressured into this. He's probably worried you're going to change—"

"Am I?" She blinked hard, trying to rid the sleep from her eyes. "I mean... am I still gonna be me?"

"Change is inevitable." The voice came from behind her. Makeda rode up on the other side of Natalie's mount. "Of course you're going to change."

"Know what else would have made you change?" Beatrice said. "Time. Fear. Chemo. Living through cancer treatment. Exposing your kids to the fear of losing you permanently."

"Life changes you," Makeda said. "In good ways and bad. Baojia will change you. You will change him. Your children will change you. Your work will change you."

"But you're never going to forget who you are," Beatrice said. "I promise. We're your friends. We won't let you."

Natalie sniffed; her nose was running. "I love you girls so much."

And that was the last thing she remembered before she fell asleep.

CHAPTER SEVEN

*N*atalie woke to the feeling of soft lips kissing along her bare shoulder. Her head hurt. Her body hurt. And her shoulder really hurt.

Whaaa?

Oh. Right.

It was still dark out, but just barely. A golden lamp shined a half light on the room. She looked over her shoulder to see a pair of deliciously bare shoulders and a familiar dark head.

"George?"

He smiled against her skin, and Natalie breathed an internal sigh of relief. Smiling Baojia meant he wasn't pissed off about the tattoo. Smiling Baojia meant that her world regained alignment.

"It's beautiful," he whispered. "Really, Red, I love it."

"It's the moon phases when—"

"When you told me you loved me the first time." He kissed the skin under the crescent moon on her right shoulder. "The moon the night Jake was born." He tapped the second. "When Sarah was born." He ran his fingers over to the fourth moon on her shoulder, the full moon. "And a full moon for when you turn."

Could she love him any more than she already did? It didn't seem possible, but he kept proving her wrong. "You remember the moon on all those dates?"

"Of course I do." He bent down and kissed her shoulder again. It still felt raw, but his lips were soft. "Those are the most important nights in my life. I love it."

"Glad you'll be able to see it every night for the next three hundred years?"

He slid over to her side. "I only get three hundred?"

Natalie turned to face him and blinked away tears. "I really love you."

"I really love you." He frowned. "I'm sorry I haven't dealt well with all this. I'm trying—"

"I know. And I know you don't like change. This is a big one, maybe the biggest we've ever been thrown. But everyone keeps telling me I'm doing the right thing. And since I'm super emotional right now, I just decided to listen to them and not myself. That way if anything goes really wrong, I can blame my friends."

He smiled, and the corners of his eyes creased. She reached over and traced the small lines that marked the geography of his face. She knew every inch of him. Every quirk and corner.

"Trust you to make a joke about all this," he said, "when I'm doing my best not to go crazy."

"It's not a joke." She put her fingers on his chin, watching his profile. "It's nothing even close to a joke. Do you think I'm not scared?" She blinked hard.

Baojia turned to look at her. "You're never scared."

"I'm scared to death." Natalie swallowed hard. "But I'm more scared of leaving you and the kids. Or getting so sick I want to die. I don't want that. I don't want to even get close to that."

He traced his finger around her lips. "You will always be hungry. You'll always crave blood. You'll learn to control it, but it will always be there, sitting in the back of your mind, like an addict craves a drug."

"The way I crave you?"

He turned to her and took her lips, kissing her hard. He hooked his arm around her waist and pulled her into his body. His hand came up to cradle her face as he thoroughly and utterly owned her kiss. She breathed into him, and he angled her head so he could go deeper.

"The sun…" She gasped for breath.

"We have time." His hunger enveloped her, and Natalie felt his amnis prick her skin like an electric charge.

Baojia pushed down the comfortable pants she'd been wearing, and Natalie kicked them off her ankles. Her shirt was already off—she'd removed it so it didn't stick to her healing tattoo—but he unhooked her bra with experienced hands and tossed it off the bed.

Her warm breasts pressed into his cool chest, and Baojia held her, slowly heating his amnis to keep her warm.

"I love that you can do that." She kissed his neck. "You're like my own personal space heater."

He was careful with her shoulder, keeping his hands off her back and rolling her up until she straddled him. He ran his hands up her body, his fingers tracing over the lumps and bumps she could be self-conscious about. He didn't see that. He didn't see any of it.

"Beautiful." His mouth said it. His eyes proved it. He watched her as she reached down and unzipped his pants, pushing them down until they were skin to skin, her thighs spread over his hips and their bodies aligned.

"We have to be quick." She glanced at the window. "This is daring for you."

Baojia surged up and caught her mouth again. He put his hands on her hips, lifted her, and Natalie sank down on him as they both let out a satisfied breath.

The corner of his mouth turned up. "I promise I won't fall asleep before you come."

"Oh no." She laughed. "You better not. I'm not rolling you to that closet, George."

His breath hitched as she began to ride him. "You're incredibly sexy."

"Am I?"

He spread his hands on the small of her back and thrust his hips up. "I'm not going to have to be so careful with you after you change."

"You mean"—she could barely form words—"this is going to get better?"

"You. Cannot. Imagine. You won't get tired." He pulled her hips down hard, going deeper than he usually did. "You won't even need to breathe."

Natalie's mouth formed the word *Fuck*, but she couldn't say it. He'd been her lover for over eight years, and he knew every button to push, every move that made her moan, every trick to bring her pleasure. Her thighs were burning, but her focus was on the growing thread of pleasure that was beginning to unspool and take hold of her body.

He caught it and coaxed her, whispering in her ear as

she closed her eyes and pressed her cheek to his. Within moments, she was coming on him, falling forward into his arms as her body shuddered and her skin came alive.

Baojia held her tight and thrust once, twice, and then he let out a long string of whispered curses in her ear as he came. He put his arms around her and fell back on the bed, his chest rising and falling against her breasts.

Natalie kissed his skin, dragged her hair across his torso like she knew he loved. She felt him shiver and then grow still.

Really, really still.

Her head popped up. "Baojia?"

His blinks were long and lazy. "Huh?"

"Uh-uh. No you don't. Come on." She scrambled off him and closed her legs tight. "No time for afterglow, George. Sun is coming up."

He blinked. "What?"

"Sun! We're not at home. You can't fall asleep here." She reached for the box of tissues on the bed and quickly cleaned herself up. "Why is sex so messy?"

His smile was lazy and wicked. "All the best things are."

She wanted to laugh, but she didn't want to encourage him. "Seriously. Darling husband of mine, father of my children, do you really want me to have to call Matt in here to move your naked ass into the closet because you fell asleep on the bed?"

That seemed to get through. "Oh. Right." He muttered something she couldn't understand and reached for a towel hanging off the chair by the small desk. "Just gonna take a shower."

"Nope." She took him by the shoulders and steered him away from the bathroom and toward the lightproof closet. "You're falling into day rest."

"What?"

"Day rest!" Natalie hooked the door with her foot and swung it open as she aimed her half-asleep vampire into the dark. "It's gonna be nice to really share a bed after I change, you know. We won't have to do this whole routine all the time."

"Routine?" He sat on the edge of the narrow bed in the walk-in closet and rubbed his eyes. "Hey." He reached for her. "Sleep with me."

"I will. I will. Give me a minute." Natalie got up to make sure the door was closed and locked, checked on the kids in their bedroom, then went back to Baojia's closet. He was already lying down and looked half-dead. She closed the door, squeezed in next to him, and pressed her face into his quickly cooling chest.

"Pretty soon, George." Closing the door shut out the light, which her slightly sore head appreciated. "Pretty soon this won't be weird at all."

Baojia didn't answer her with anything intelligible, but his arm wrapped around her waist and he fell completely still.

Baojia woke the next night and smelled sunscreen, water, sweaty children, and blood. He turned to see a thermos sitting next to him, which proved to be the source of the blood.

He opened it and sniffed.

Great. Cattle blood. He'd forgotten that most of Carwyn's clan kept to his human-free diet.

Wait. Cattle. Cattle blood could be a problem.

Frowning, he drank down the cow blood and rose, only to realize he was buck-naked.

Oh right. He wrapped the towel around his waist and walked out of the closet and into the bedroom where wet bathing suits and beach towels decorated every available surface. He didn't hear or see his wife, so he assumed she was with the children. He took a quick shower, dressed, and walked out of the room and into the hall.

Following the high-pitched voices, he walked down the stairs and into the great room where the children were decorating cookies. Or doing something that involved green frosting and sprinkles everywhere.

"Baojia!" Dez waved. "You're the first one awake."

He raised an eyebrow and headed toward his son, who had something green in his hair. "Clearly not." He took a napkin and tried to remove the green gunk. "Frosting goes on the cookies, not the hair, Jake."

Jake looked up. "Oh. Hi, Dad!" He reached up and touched his hair with green-coated hands. "I have frosting in my hair?"

"It appears you have frosting everywhere."

"Baba!" He turned to the sound of Sarah's voice, only to find her halfway up the stone fireplace in the center of the room.

"Hello, Monkey." Baojia walked over and took Matt's place underneath the climbing girl. "Did you ask Isabel if it was okay to climb the fireplace?"

"Mama climbed rocks today!"

Matt and Baojia exchanged a look.

"Of course she did," Baojia muttered.

"She did great," Matt said. "She's a natural."

"Don't encourage her."

Matt grinned. "The wife or the daughter?"

"Either." Parenting a small daredevil was a tricky proposition. Baojia never wanted to clip Sarah's wings or make her think he didn't have confidence in her.

But sometimes wings that were only four *needed* to be clipped. "Can you climb down, please?"

Her mouth formed a small *O*. "Ummm…"

"Not sure how to do that?"

Her smile would have been adorable if it weren't so guilty. "Can you get me?"

"No."

"Baba!"

"But I'll show you how to get down." He climbed on the hearth and reached for her little legs. "Which rock did you put your foot on to get up?"

"I don't know."

"Feel around," he said. "Don't let go, and feel with your toes."

Bit by bit, he worked Sarah down the rocks until she was standing on her own feet with her hands fisted in the air. "I did it!"

"You definitely did." He picked her up and put her on his hip as they walked back into the kitchen. "Did you decorate cookies?" He was guessing yes by the red frosting smeared on her cheek.

"Yes." She pointed at some red stars. "See those?"

"With all the sprinkles?"

She nodded.

They were truly a sight to behold. Sarah's cookies bore a thick coating of red frosting made even thicker by colored sugar and sprinkles. "That looks... very sweet, Sarah."

The huge smile she gave him made his heart beat. "Do you want to taste one?"

Please no. "We need to save them for Christmas, don't we?"

"Okay." She crawled down from his arms and onto a chair, reaching for the most sprinkled cookie. "But I'm going to tell everyone to save this one for you."

"Thank you... so much." He ruffled Jake's still-gloopy hair and asked, "Has anyone seen Uncle Lucien?"

"I think he's still in his cabin," Matt said. "You're the only vampire awake so far."

"Mom says Dad is an early riser," Sarah said. "Early and *often*."

Baojia coughed and Matt snorted a laugh.

"I bet she does say that," Matt said.

"Shut up," Baojia muttered. "Do you know if Lucien brought *supplies*?"

Matt frowned. "What?"

Baojia lowered his voice. "I had cattle blood when I woke up tonight. Do you know if Lucien brought *supplies*?"

"Oh, you mean..." Matt's eyes went wide. "I didn't even think of that."

"Tonight was the first night I needed blood since we've been here," Baojia said quietly. "I just thought of it too."

"Unless Lucien planned ahead and brought some of the genuine article…"

"We could have a serious problem."

Cattle blood was not going to cut it for a newborn vampire. Not even close. If Lucien didn't have the blood issue covered, Natalie's turning could mean a very unhappy New Year.

CHAPTER EIGHT

"*D*on't overreact." Lucien tried to calm his pacing friend. "We have blood, and we have time. We can get more."

Giovanni spoke from the doorway. "I'll have the pilot fly to Santiago immediately. We have connections at a blood bank there. Baojia, we'll get enough stores for her."

"See?" Lucien nodded. "We'll take care of her."

Baojia wasn't satisfied. He paced Lucien's cabin like a caged cat. "But what will we do in the long term? In the first week alone, she could easily drink the equivalent of four human beings. We all know how newborns eat. If she slipped up even once, she'd be devastated."

It hadn't even occurred to Lucien that their hosts would be animal drinkers, that Carwyn's austere diet would extend to his family. It wasn't just the initial week, it was every week after. They could get reserves for a while, but eventually Natalie would need regular, fresh donors.

"Would the humans in the valley be willing to donate blood?" Lucien asked Giovanni.

He shrugged. "I've never asked."

"Beatrice—"

"We hunted in the nearby villages. We went into town. We had stores here."

"Ernesto sent regular shipments," Baojia said. "I remember that."

"And we were exchanging blood," Giovanni added. "Which—I don't want to presume—but it's possible you and Natalie will also choose to do."

Baojia frowned. "That makes a difference?"

Lucien nodded. "A huge one." He thought of how quickly Makeda had started to control her power and her appetites once she began taking his vein. In addition to control, it was an intensely pleasurable and intimate experience to exchange blood with one's mate.

But he didn't need to get into that with Baojia.

"Good." The worried husband was nodding. "At least that's *something* I can do. Natalie can drain me dry if she wants to."

Lucien saw the moment Baojia realized how much he wanted Natalie to do that. The quiet vampire stared at the wall intently. Then he cleared his throat, crossed his arms, and looked out the window.

Not many could read Baojia, but Lucien had spent years in close proximity with him as they worked and lived together. Their friendship had been a surprise to both of them, but not an unwelcome one.

"Okay." Baojia nodded. "Okay. We can do this."

"And supplementing with animal blood will not affect

her long-term health," Lucien said. "Remember, she's going to be my daughter. And I have not sired a child in a very, very long time. My blood is rich."

And he was more than willing to share it with Natalie. In truth, he already felt deep affection toward the woman, possibly because this change had been planned for so long. Lucien didn't feel like a father toward her, but an older brother? Yes, it felt a little like that.

Giovanni said, "All things considered, it's likely Natalie will be stronger than you once she gains control."

Lucien asked, "Is that going to bother you?"

Baojia rolled his eyes. "She's already stronger than me. She just has different ways of showing it." He turned and walked out of Lucien's cabin. "Come up to the house when you're finished talking," he said. "The kids made cookies, and Gus and Matt are barbecuing."

CHRISTMAS EVE PASSED IN A BLUR OF FOOD AND LAUGHTER and presents. Much to everyone's delight, Isabel, Gus, and the rest of the family were excellent musicians and the evening concluded with a dance in the great room. All the sofas and chairs were pushed to the side while flutes, guitars, and drums came out. Isabel and one of Gus's nieces sang ballads, but most of the music was fast, and the children and adults enjoyed the dance.

"Mama, look!" Sarah yelled from the dance floor where Lucien had put the little girl on his shoulders and was spinning her around. Sarah held out her arms and laughed long and loud.

"Look how tall you are!" Natalie's heart was nearly bursting.

"I know!"

Lucien grinned, his normally solemn face transformed by the small child on his shoulders. Sarah had that gift. Everyone fell in love with her even if they were also exasperated.

Natalie's belly was full of roasted wild turkey, and she leaned against Baojia's chest, his arms wrapped tightly around her as they watched their friends and children dancing.

Dez had overseen the best American Thanksgiving dinner ever produced in Patagonia. There were mashed potatoes and apple pie. Lots of turkey and rich cornbread dressing spiked with salty bacon. The only thing missing had been cranberry sauce, but since that was Natalie's least favorite part of Thanksgiving dinner, she was okay with that.

She'd checked nearly everything off on "Nat's Bucket O' Blood List." She'd gone rock climbing with some of Gus's nephews, who'd led her up a popular trail and managed to get Dez and Natalie—neither of whom had ever climbed before—in harnesses and up the side of a small cliff. It was thrilling and hard and probably not that safe, but she hadn't told her husband that and neither had the boys, for which she was eternally grateful.

She'd been exhausted. She'd also felt more alive than she had in years.

Natalie and Dez borrowed kayaks and took all the kids down the river for a picnic. They played in the sun and sand every day. Her tattoo was healing nicely, and it didn't hurt at all anymore.

Wine had definitely been drunk.

"How are you feeling?" Baojia kissed the top of her head. "Christmas is tomorrow."

"Technically"—she looked at her watch—"Christmas is now."

He frowned. "Did we pack the kids' stockings?"

"We did."

He nuzzled her neck. "You are extraordinary."

"Because I remembered to bring the kids' Christmas stockings?"

"Because…" He took a deep breath and fell silent.

Natalie looked over her shoulder. "Baojia?"

He was struggling to find words. Natalie put a hand on his jaw and pressed her cheek to his chest. Her beautiful, quiet man. "It's okay. I know."

She did know. She knew his heart. He showed it in a thousand different ways. He showed his heart when he programmed the coffee maker before he retired to day rest. He showed it by being so patient with the kids when Natalie lost her temper. He showed her in all the ways he supported her work, which was so much a part of her identity. For the six hours a night that he was able to share with his children, they were the center of his world. He'd learned how to cook so he could feed them food he would never eat. He ate green vegetables to set a good example.

"You are extraordinary for reasons you cannot even imagine," he said quietly.

"So are you."

He reached up and twisted her hair around his finger. "I don't want your eyes to change. I love your eyes."

She smiled. "I'm hoping they'll stay the same too, but if they don't, is it really a big deal?"

"No."

"Nope." She slid her arm around his waist. "I hope you still smell as good when I have a super nose."

His chest shook with quiet laughter. "Me too."

She looked up and he met her eyes. "Hey, George?"

"Hey, Red."

"I really love you."

"I really love you too."

"And I would not want to do this with anyone but you."

"Same." His mouth tightened into a line. "You sure you're all right?"

"I will be." She nodded with more confidence than she felt. After all, if there was one thing she didn't need to do, it was freak out. Christmas was tomorrow. If it was going to be her last Christmas morning, she wanted to stay up to see the dawn.

BRIGID AND CARWYN SAT OUT ON THE PORCH, WATCHING the sky grow lighter and lighter.

"Do you remember that Christmas morning?" Carwyn asked.

"Hmm?" Brigid sipped a mug of tea. "Which one?"

"Purple hair."

His glorious girl. Carwyn watched the smile spread across her face, and it was his own personal sunrise.

"In Wicklow when I was still human?" She nodded. "I do remember that. Was I smoking?"

"Aye."

"Oof." She winced. "Such a bad girl."

"My bad girl." He hooked his hand around her thigh. "I was thinking of that tonight."

"Was it my last Christmas before I changed?" Brigid narrowed her eyes. "I don't think so."

"Maybe the last with the family."

"Maybe." She swayed in one of the hardwood rockers Carwyn and Gus had made for the porch. "What has you thinking of that?"

"Natalie."

"Oh, but she'll have *so* many more Christmases," Brigid said. "She can't see it now for all the worry, but all the important things are going to stay the same. And she'll be so much safer. So much happier in the end. She might not enjoy food as much. But that's it really."

"And watching the sunrise." He nodded toward the horizon. "There's that."

"The sun." Brigid shrugged. "It's overrated."

Carwyn laughed.

"What?" Brigid said. "It is. And they have those lovely nature programs on the telly now. She can watch those if she misses the sun."

"There is that."

"I mean, I feel for the lot of you who lived before television and movies. I can say that for certain. But now?"

"We deserve no pity," Carwyn said. "I agree completely."

"Oh, now I didn't say I don't pity you, poor man. You've got that troublesome smoker of a wife to put up with." She winked.

"You're right. My eternity is blighted."

She reached over and tried to punch his thigh, but he laughed and intercepted her.

"Blighted, he says," she muttered. "I'll blight you."

"I'm sure you will."

Brigid stood and moved from her chair to Carwyn's lap. He wrapped his arm around the tiny woman and rested his chin on her shoulder. "Darling girl."

"Sweet man."

"Happy Christmas."

"Happy Christmas. I'm glad she's here. Glad Natalie is here. This is a good place, even if it has far too many people."

"Ah, my small, unsociable urchin, I love you so."

"I love you too, *carnín*."

Natalie waited for the sunrise, waited for the children to collapse into bed and for Baojia to fall asleep in his lightproof room before she walked outside, sat in the sun, and allowed herself to fall apart.

Everyone was sleeping, and she was looking at an eternity of darkness. In the silence of the dawn light, she allowed herself to grieve. She grieved for the sunlight and the passing of time. She grieved for the passing of change and her humanity.

But mostly she grieved for the year of life she would miss. She'd been watching Carina and Jake that night, watching the differences between ten-year-old, preteen Carina and Jake's still rounded baby face and innocent eyes. The time passed so swiftly, and while a year might not seem like a lot to a century-old vampire, for a child it was an eternity.

It was a year of school and countless tiny memories.

It was a school crush and a new best friend.

It was new words and new books and new discoveries she wouldn't be a part of.

Her chest felt hollow and her head was too full.

"Natalie?"

She heard Dez's voice behind her, and she swiftly straightened and wiped her tears.

"Don't." Dez came and sat beside her, wrapping her arms around Natalie. "Don't do that. You cry if you want to. This is a lot, and you've been putting on a brave face for a month now."

"A…" She hiccupped. "A y-year, Dez. A whole year, and I'm not gonna be able to see my babies. I can't… I can't handle that. I can't even imagine it."

"You *will* handle it." Dez squeezed her shoulders fiercely. "You will survive it, and they will too. They will have a father who adores them, and they will have good people around them. People you trust. People who love them."

"B-but will they understand?" She sniffed and wiped her eyes. "Will they understand why I can't be there if they're hurt? If they're sad? What if something really bad happens and I'm not there?"

"But you will be there," Dez said. "You will be. Even if you can't be right next to them. You'll be thinking of them, praying for them, talking with them when you're feeling like yourself again."

Natalie tried to nod. "I-I know all that, but Sarah is so young, and she—"

"You will be there for them." Dez shook her. "Don't you see that? This is what you have to do to stay with them. This is a short sacrifice for a long reward. And they will understand that later if they don't understand now."

"B-Baojia didn't want to tell them about the cancer. We haven't told them because… we figured it would be bad to scare them when it wasn't going to be an issue, so we've just been telling them that it's time for Mom to become a vampire and that's why we're here, but are they going to think I did this just because? That I'm abandoning—"

"No." Dez shook her again. "No, they're not going to think you're abandoning them. Natalie." She laughed a little. "They're going to talk to you every night. You'll have phone calls. Maybe even video chatting if the signal booster thing Matt is trying out works."

Dez pointed at the house. "Know what Beatrice is doing right now? She's inside with Giovanni, waiting to talk to Ben in Mongolia for Christmas. Mongolia! Natalie, your kids are right here, surrounded by wonderful, safe, caring people. They are going to be fine."

She took deep breaths, trying to calm the ache in her heart. "Okay." She nodded. "Okay." Leaning her head on Dez, she said, "Sorry for the freak-out."

"Are you kidding? You've been the one calming everyone else down about all this for a month now. I know you've been putting on a brave face to convince Baojia and Lucien you're just fine with all this, but you don't have to pretend with your friends. You want to be scared? Be scared. You want to freak out that you're gonna have fangs? Freak out a little. I mean… do it now when you don't have fangs so I don't have to worry about you biting me."

Natalie swallowed the lump in her throat and checked her pockets for anything she could blow her nose with. A half-shredded napkin with green frosting smeared on it would have to do.

"I'm really worried I'm going to be a bad vampire. Is that weird?"

Dez snorted. "What?"

"I mean, everyone I know who's a vampire is way more serious and badass than I am. I don't know how to fire a gun. I mean, I could if I had to, but the pen is mightier than the sword, right? In my heart, I'm a total pacifist. Can a pacifist even be a vampire? Is that ideologically consistent, Dez?"

Dez pursed her lips. "Well…"

"Be honest. Can you even imagine me beating someone up?" She thought about some of the assignments she'd been on. "I mean, it's sheer luck I'm still alive at all. I run out into traffic."

Dez put her hand on Natalie's shoulder. "I have a one-word answer to this conundrum: Carwyn."

"No, that doesn't count! Because have you seen him? He acts all ha-ha-jokester, but when he gets really mad, he can be scary as hell. I've seen it." She put a hand on her chest. "I don't have that thing. Whatever it is he has, the thing that Baojia and Giovanni and Beatrice have? I don't have that. I don't."

"Does Makeda?"

Natalie cocked her head. "I don't know."

"I mean, Mak's a scientist. She's not bloodthirsty or badass, but she's managed."

Natalie nodded. "Okay. Okay, maybe. But I still say—"

"I say that you don't have to have all this figured out in the beginning," Dez said. "All I'm saying is that if Carwyn the priest and Makeda the nerdy doctor can figure out a way to be themselves through eternity, then you can too." She squeezed Natalie's arm. "I know it."

CHAPTER NINE

"You can't be there." Giovanni's voice was unwavering. "Your instincts won't allow it."

"I'm not leaving her." Baojia didn't blink. "I don't know how you even think it would be possible."

Christmas night had come and gone. Dinner had been glorious, but everyone was exhausted from the night before, and Natalie had gone to bed early, curled up with the children in the big bed in their room. She wanted to wake up early with them to watch the sunrise. It would be their last sunrise with their mother. The next night, Natalie would make the change to become a vampire.

"Think," Beatrice said. "Lucien will be draining Natalie's blood to the point of death. You know him. He is your closest friend. But the fact is, she is your wife. Your mate. And what he's going to do *will* harm her, even though you know—in your logical mind—it's necessary."

Lucien took a deep breath. "My friend, I agree with them."

"Even though I couldn't stop Beatrice's father from

turning her, I completely ignited watching it," Giovanni said. "You must remember."

Baojia said, "You reacted that way because she didn't tell you she was doing it. Which in retrospect—by the way —I am completely on your side." He turned to Beatrice. "I don't know what you were thinking."

Beatrice gave him a withering look. "I see the Society of Affronted Husbands has decided to make an appearance. I am not rehashing this with you."

Baojia turned to Lucien. "You didn't overreact when I turned Makeda." He glanced at Makeda, who was reading in the corner of the library. "You were completely calm. Clinical even."

"Different," Makeda murmured. "Totally different."

"Agreed." Lucien exchanged a look with his mate. "Though I had feelings for Makeda from the beginning, I wasn't in love with her. I didn't have eight years together and two children, Baojia. It's not the same thing."

Giovanni said, "When Beatrice turned, I was incredibly angry that she hadn't allowed me to be with her. In hindsight, I know it was for the best." He leaned forward. "*Think.* Your instincts are going to tell you that Lucien is killing her. Do you want to lose control when doing so could have such horrendous consequences?"

"I don't want to fight you off when I need to be taking care of Natalie," Lucien said. "You need to think of her."

Makeda spoke quietly. "She won't want you there."

Baojia blinked. "What?"

Makeda had been quiet throughout the discussion in the library. Beatrice, Lucien, Giovanni, and Baojia were discussing the mechanics of the change, and Makeda had been sitting quietly in the corner, reading her book and sipping a glass of wine.

"She won't want you there." Makeda set her book to the side. "But she won't tell you to stay away because she loves you. She's your wife, but she is an independent person. This change is her choice. It is her body. Lucien will be her sire. Fundamentally, this is not about you. I imagine she would rather you stay with Sarah and Jake, not with her."

Baojia sat back and let Makeda's words sink in. Though he was Makeda's sire, he had never considered her a child, even in the vampire sense. She was too mature. Too wise. He had an enormous amount of affection for her, but she was more like a sister than a child.

"Do you truly think so?"

"I do."

Baojia took a deep breath and felt a little bit of his heart break off. He knew Makeda was right. This was Natalie's decision. Natalie's future. Her future was entwined with his, but it did not belong to him. "I'll stay with Sarah and Jake."

Lucien put a hand on his shoulder. "Trust me."

"I do."

"And be there when she wakes," Giovanni said. "That's the most disorienting time. That's when she'll need you the most."

He looked at Lucien. "Tell me what to expect."

"Do you dislike being dirty?"

"As in…?"

"Actually being in dirt. Having dirt on your skin."

"I don't know that I *like* it, but it doesn't particularly bother me."

"Good." Lucien smiled. "That is very good news."

NATALIE WATCHED THE SUNRISE WITH JAKE AND SARAH BY her side. "You guys understand what's going to happen tonight, right?"

Sarah leaned against her, bundled up in blankets and snuggling under Natalie's arm. "You're gonna be like Daddy, and we won't get to see you during the day anymore."

"No, you won't," Natalie said. "Does that make you sad?"

"If you're sleeping and Baba's sleeping, who's gonna take care of us?" Sarah said. "Ariel and Miss Olivia aren't here!"

"Well, right now they're taking care of everything back at home. But they may be coming soon, and while we're here, Beatrice will help take care of you. And Dema—"

"I like Dema!" Sarah bounced up. "Can Dema come to our house?"

"Don't be stupid," Jake said. "Who would take care of Sadia?"

"Hey." Natalie pinched his arm. "Don't say stupid."

"Sorry." Jake was pouting. "How long until we can see you?"

"Dad told you."

"A year?" Jake's eyes were wide. "Really a year?"

"Why?" Sarah started crawling into Natalie's lap. "A year is for*ever*, Mama."

"It's not forever." Natalie smoothed the flyaway curls

from Sarah's face. "It's a long time, but I'm going to need that long to feel like myself again. To get better."

"Are you sick?"

"Kind of." She kissed Sarah's head and hugged Jake closer. "But after I become a vampire, I won't be sick ever. Isn't that good news?"

"Did Dad have to spend that long away from his family too?"

Natalie took a deep breath. "I think it was a lot longer."

Jake's eyes went wide. "Longer than a year?"

"Yeah." She glanced at him. "See? A year isn't so bad."

"I'm gonna be taller," Jake said. "Maybe as tall as Andre."

"Maybe." Natalie smiled. "I think you're gonna be pretty tall. Like Grandpa Ellis."

Andre was one of Gus and Isabel's many nephews. Or great-nephews? Great-great-nephews? Who knew? He was one of the kids on the ranch and he was a few years older than Jake, but he'd been happy to have someone near his age to play with. He and Jake had quickly become friends.

"Mom, does Grandpa Ellis know what's happening?" Jake put a hand on her arm. "Did you tell him?"

Jake understood more than Sarah why they couldn't spend much time with Grandpa Ellis, though they did talk via screen time. "We haven't told Grandpa Ellis, baby. We'll video chat when it's safe. He just knows we're out of the country for a while."

In fact, they'd told Natalie's father that they'd be out of the country for a year for Baojia's work. Since Natalie's father had never truly recovered from his wife's death, Natalie's contact with him had always been sporadic and limited. Her becoming a vampire would just make it more so.

"What do you want to do today?" She hugged both her children close. "Anything you want."

"I want to… make cookies. And play with my new paints," Sarah said.

"Cookies sound good." Jake shrugged. "Whatever you want to do, Mom."

He was already so much like his father it made her heart ache. Jake wanted everyone to be safe and happy. If everyone around him was happy, he was happy. If someone was troubled, he was troubled. He had a protective streak a mile wide and a huge heart.

Natalie kissed the top of Jake's head. "I'm gonna miss you so much."

"But you'll be back." Jake slipped his hand in hers. "A year is gonna go really fast, Mom."

"Yeah." Sarah put her arms around Natalie's neck. "Super-duper fast."

THEY WAITED UNTIL BOTH THE CHILDREN WERE SLEEPING. She and Baojia put them to bed together in Natalie and Baojia's bed, giving kisses, reading stories, and getting many cups of water. It was an early bedtime for both kids, but they were tired out from a long, happy day of playing in the river, baking cookies, and painting sunny pictures for Natalie to take with her to the cabin.

Baojia took her hand when both the children were in bed and led her to the door. Natalie lingered, watching their chests rise and fall. She stared at them for a long time, matching her breath to theirs.

"Make me leave." She blinked back tears. "Otherwise I never will."

He put his arms around her from behind and rested his chin on her shoulder. "You're doing this for them."

"And for you." She leaned into him. "And for me."

"Look as long as you want to," he said. "And remember that a year is going to fly by."

She nodded, but she couldn't tear her eyes away. She gripped his hands in hers. "They're safe here."

"So safe," he said. "Surrounded by our family. They will wake up in the morning while you are sleeping, and Dema will take them swimming. Beatrice will be in the library to read them stories. Matt will take them on the horses, and Dez will bake cookies."

Natalie nodded, but she still couldn't look away.

"And when it's bedtime, Carwyn will come in and say prayers with them and let Jake pray for the entire human race and all the aliens too."

She laughed through her tears.

"Giovanni will probably try to teach them Latin. Brigid will give Jake archery lessons because I told her a seven-year-old handling a BB gun was out of the question. And Makeda and Lucien will be there from sundown to sunup, making sure they both feel like they're at home."

She nodded and sniffed. "Okay." She turned and stood in his arms, letting his strength soak into her fear. "Okay."

"One more kiss for now," he said. "Then we'll go."

She nodded, walked quickly to the bed, and kissed Sarah's cheek. Then she kissed Jake's and reminded herself that her children were loved, and after that night, not even cancer could take her away from them.

BAOJIA AND NATALIE WALKED THROUGH THE WOODS AND UP the narrow trail to a large, spacious cabin built into the hills around the valley.

"Holy shit." Natalie stopped when it came into view. "You know, I forget a lot of the time that they're totally loaded."

"This is… impressive. And to be fair, we're also loaded, but not as loaded as they are, and we have two children to send to college."

"What you're saying is when it's time for us to build our chalet in the Patagonia Mountains, we'll keep it a little more modest?"

"I mean…" He shrugged. "Is that third story strictly necessary?"

"It's a little ostentatious."

"So it fits the Italian." Baojia grinned when she elbowed him. "Kidding. Kind of."

Beatrice came out on the porch. "We can hear you!"

Baojia laughed as Natalie covered her eyes. "Stupid vampire hearing."

He put his arm around her. "You'll get used to it soon enough."

Natalie turned to him. "Hey, George—"

"I know." He put his hands on her waist and faced her. "I'm leaving you here. I'm not going to follow. This step… it's for you to take."

She took a deep breath and swallowed hard. "Stay with the kids?"

"I will." He studied her face, every inch of it lit clearly by the full moon hanging over the valley. "Thank you."

She smiled. "For what?"

"For loving me. You knew this day was coming. From the beginning, you knew. And you loved me anyway."

Natalie threw her arms around his neck. "It wasn't a choice."

He squeezed her tight. "Yes. It was."

Baojia took her mouth in one last searing kiss before he sped away into the night.

Natalie watched him go. Then she turned and walked up the path to the light waiting for her. Makeda and Lucien were in the doorway. Lucien, smiling with his timeless eyes, and Makeda, welcoming her with open arms.

Beatrice met her at the foot of the stairs and held out her hands. "Are you ready?"

Natalie looked around her, at the living night that called her, the moon and the wind, the soaring mountains surrounding them like an ancient embrace. She looked over her shoulder at the lights in the valley below.

"I'm ready."

CHAPTER TEN

*S*he woke in a bed, but it wasn't like any bed she'd felt before. She was surrounded by warmth and energy. Her body felt like it was part of the bed, connected like something plugged in to a vast energy source.

She took a deep breath and smelled earth and green living things. She was naked, but it felt like the most natural thing in the world.

Her throat burned with hunger.

She opened her eyes and wondered what had happened to them. She felt him in the darkness that wasn't dark, his scent as familiar as her own.

"Baojia?"

"Drink." He held a cup to her lips, and she drank. It soothed the burning in her throat, but the taste was too rich, like asking for water and being given a glass of wine.

"Mmph." She pushed the cup away. "Too much."

"What?"

She shook her head and the world spun around her.

Too much input. Too fast. She closed her eyes. "Too much."

"Keep your eyes closed." He moved next to her, and she felt the heat from his body.

No, not heat. Energy. Pure, undiluted energy.

A shiver of excitement coursed through her.

"You need to drink."

"It's too much."

"You barely drank a pint." His voice stayed soft but firm. "You need more."

"I need…" What did she need? She opened her eyes and looked for him. Focused on him. "You."

His smile was glorious. "Hello, wife."

"Hi." Oh, he was even more handsome than before. His brown eyes were flecked with dark onyx and gold. The angles of his cheekbones were elegant. Had the shadows always highlighted his features so well? His scent was layered with the smells of water. Minerals and vegetation. Rich grasses, salt, and sand.

He leaned forward and kissed her mouth gently. An aching sprang in her jaws, and a rush of desire bolted through her like lightning. She tasted blood and tentatively moved her tongue through her mouth.

"I haf fanks." She covered her mouth. "Oh my gah."

His low chuckle echoed around the dark room. "Yes, you do. They're very beautiful."

"You think so?" She felt like she'd just had the strangest dental work ever and her mouth was half numb. Only it wasn't numb, and her throat was burning again.

She reached for the cup. "More."

The rich liquid hit her tongue, coating her mouth and

soothing her throat. Her fangs retracted. The burning dulled.

Natalie looked around her. "Where are we?"

"We're in a room that Lucien just happened to dig into the back of Giovanni's house while you were sleeping." He craned his neck. "It's pretty nice actually. They can probably use it as a wine cellar or something when we're done with it."

Natalie recognized the darkness, but it was as if she'd been given an extra set of eyes. She saw everything. The smooth dirt floor and the stone walls. The soft bed she'd felt so comfortable in was a shallow bed of earth that had been churned up to surround her body.

"Did Lucien... I'm trying really hard not to feel like this is a shallow grave, but it kinda is, George." She flexed her fingers and her toes. "Except the shallow grave feels supergood. Like that feeling of jumping into the pool the first day of summer."

"He said it would be the easiest way for you to wake. That you'd be most comfortable here. Was he right?"

"I think so?" She shuffled her shoulders into the bed of dirt and felt the ground form around her. "Whoa, that is so weird. How am I doing that?"

Baojia smiled. "That would be a question for Lucien."

"Did you wake up— Whoa." She sat up. "More blood."

"Good." He held out the cup for her to drink, and Natalie swallowed gulp after gulp of the thick liquid.

"Oh, I really do not like that, but I do." She licked her lips and tasted earth and iron. "You drink that every day?"

"It's blood, Red. I drink it about two times a week. You know that."

"Right." She swallowed hard. "I mean, it feels good, but it doesn't taste good."

He frowned. "Really?" He took a tentative sip from the cup. "Tastes normal to me."

"Ugh." She made a face. "Really?"

"Really." The frown stayed. "So... wait. This doesn't taste good to you? Not at all?"

"No. I mean, I want it, but it doesn't taste good." She took another long drink. "What is it?"

"This is normal human blood. Donated. It's fresh even. We saved the preserved blood for when you needed it later. This is from... Well, it's from a willing donor."

She waved a hand. "Yeah, maybe don't tell me that right now." Her skin prickled and itched. It didn't feel bad, just... "I don't know how I'm feeling right now."

"That's perfectly normal." His fingers tentatively ran over her bare shoulder. "Do you remember last night?"

"If only you were asking me that because I got rip-roaring drunk instead of having all the blood drained from my body." She shook her head. "I don't remember much actually."

"That's not uncommon."

"I remember Lucien biting me, which was weird. And like... not sexy at all. He's such a doctor."

"Yes, he is."

"And then I remember... I think I just fell asleep. Did he use amnis on me?"

"I believe so. It soothes the normal human reactions to having the blood drained from your body."

She put a hand to her forehead and closed her eyes again. "Wow. Yeah. Superweird." The burning in her throat spiked, and she felt her fangs grow long. "Oh my gah. More blooh. I nee more blooh."

This time, Natalie drank and she didn't stop. She couldn't. She drank and drank and the blood didn't taste good, but it was satisfying. So much more satisfying than anything she had ever drunk in her entire life, and she just needed a river of it poured directly into her mouth like a waterfall of bloody goodness.

After she'd drunk what felt like the entire weight of her body and more, she took a breath. "Oh, that's so weird."

"What?" Baojia was cleaning off her face with a warm, wet cloth.

"I don't feel full. I mean, I kind of do, but mostly I just feel…"

"Hmm?" He was intent on his work, dabbing at her face and lips, trying not to rub her sensitive skin.

Natalie felt her fangs drop hard, but her throat wasn't burning. She stared at Baojia's mouth, the fine curve of his upper lip. Her eyes trailed to his neck. His shoulder. They dropped down to the line of dark hair that ran down his belly, and an unrecognizable sound left her throat.

He stopped what he was doing and met her eyes. "Did you just growl at me?"

Natalie tackled him.

She took his mouth and straddled his body, her thighs pressing into his hips. "Take off your pants."

"Mmmph." He couldn't speak, but he shoved her back and stood, tearing off the pants he'd been wearing.

Natalie stared. His body was covered in dirt, but his erection stood proudly, jutting out from his body. Natalie eyed it and her mouth watered.

He walked toward her and tapped her chin. "Uh-uh. Not until you've got a little more control with those fangs, Red."

She gripped his hips and ran her tongue up the inside of his thigh, scraping her fangs along his skin and leaving a red, welling line of blood.

"Oh fuck." He breathed out hard. "You gonna lick that up?"

She couldn't answer him, but she did as he suggested, and the spike of pleasure that hit her tongue felt like an electric charge.

The blood in the cup had been thick, rich, and heavy. His blood was sweet.

Baojia knelt down and faced her. His hands cupped her breasts, and she let her head fall back. It felt so good. Everywhere he touched felt so good. She wanted him to touch her everywhere.

"Like this?" He sent a wave of amnis licking over her body.

Had she said that aloud? Natalie moaned. It felt so good she wanted to weep.

"Yes, you said that aloud. What about this?" His mouth touched her neck. His lips explored his favorite place to bite, and her body responded instinctively. "Do you want this, Natalie?"

"Yes, yes, yes." She loved it when he bit her. "But first..." She put a hand on his erection.

"Excellent idea." He laid her back on the ground, spread her legs, and eased his way inside.

Her flesh was swollen and ready for him. She wrapped her legs around his hips, thrilling at the surge of energy she felt at her back.

Plugged in. She felt like she'd been plugged in and turned on at the same time.

He angled her hips up and went deeper as his fangs pierced her neck.

Without any warning or buildup, Natalie climaxed in a massive, overwhelming wave. Baojia didn't stop moving in her. He thrust through her climax and into it, holding her as she shuddered and wept.

Her mouth felt empty. Her fangs ached.

"Here." He kept moving, but he put his hand at the back of her head and brought her mouth to his neck. He turned his head and bared the side of his throat to her.

Natalie didn't have to be told twice. She hooked her leg over his hips and drew him even deeper as she struck his neck with her fangs and latched on.

His roar of pleasure echoed in the stone chamber.

She held on and sucked hard, swallowing the sweet blood in ravenous gulps.

This was sex. What they'd been doing for the past eight years had only been foreplay.

He convulsed in her arms, and she felt his climax as it if were her own. His blood mingled with hers. His amnis —cool, precise, and deadly—entered her body and twisted around her wild, chaotic energy.

He surrounded her and she grew calm.

This.

This.

This was her mate. Her lover. Her husband. The other half of her soul.

She understood it now. Her blood and body worshipped him. His touch adored her.

Natalie didn't have any words. Not a single one could even touch the measure of her feelings.

He was everything. And she finally understood.

S**HE WAS EVERYTHING**.

Baojia watched Natalie as she drifted in a postcoital haze. She'd drunk more stored blood and fallen into a semiconscious trance, sinking back into the bed of earth Lucien had prepared for her. He could feel her amnis in his body and knew that it was chaotic and confused. But it was also happy. Content.

Wild and happy. Confused and content.

Yes, he knew this woman.

He couldn't contain his smile. He felt like he might be smiling for centuries. So much for the stoic and cynical enforcer; he might have to find a new line of work.

He played with her hair and watched her face. Every tiny hint of expression was a new wonder. What was she thinking? Was she cold? Warm? Hungry?

They were both completely filthy, but she didn't seem to care at all. He would have to adjust his thinking. For her, being in the earth would be as soothing and familiar as the water was for him. The grit wouldn't bother her skin any more than seawater bothered his. It would be an adjustment for someone as fastidious as Baojia, but he would happily adapt, especially if getting dirty resulted in that level of sex on a regular basis.

Relieved. That's what he felt. He was massively relieved.

Her eyes hadn't changed. They were still the same

clear blue that reminded him of sun-splashed water. Her laugh was the same. Her awkwardness and her honesty. She still craved his bite. Plus he no longer had to be painfully and carefully gentle when they made love.

Baojia felt as randy as a sixteen-year-old boy.

"Hey, George?" Her voice was drowsy.

"Yes, Natalie?"

"I really love you."

"I really love you too."

"Can we just have lots and lots sex for an entire year?"

His laugh started low and got louder, filling the room. "I forgot how newborns tend to have a one-track mind."

"Yeah, okay, but can we?"

"We can stay in here for a few nights at least. After that, you might want to explore the outside world."

"I don't know." She turned toward him, and her fangs were down again. "The outside world can be really overrated."

CHAPTER ELEVEN

"Are they gonna be weird if my fangs come out?"

"They love the fangs."

"Are you sure?"

"Trust me, the kids love the fangs. You're gonna end up showing them over and over until your jaw aches." Baojia kissed her temple. "Just relax."

It had been two weeks since Natalie had changed, and she finally felt steady enough to hold a normal conversation. They had kept her stimuli simple for the first week. She and Baojia slept in the stone room on the ground, the earthen floor Lucien had built literally grounding her chaotic emotions and reactions.

The second week, they'd moved to a room in the far back of the house that jutted up to bedrock. Lucien and Makeda stayed in the house with them. They ate together. Played card games and watched movies. She was distractible and erratic, moved to tears in a heartbeat and snapping with anger over minor things.

Natalie likened it to the absolute worst case of PMS

she'd ever had. Only on steroids. Lucien and Baojia were confused, but Makeda backed her up.

Toward the end of the second week, she felt steadier, but she still hadn't ventured any farther than the porch. She felt inundated by her senses anytime she stepped outside. Baojia thought it might help to remind her why she needed to wrestle control back, so he arranged for his Nocht-compatible tablet to be brought to the cabin, and Giovanni and Beatrice would wait on the other end with the kids.

The signal booster Matt had installed seemed to be working if they sat on the far corner of the porch, so Natalie and Baojia waited to connect with the two people they missed the most.

The tablet beeped as it connected, and a picture of two small chins appeared on the screen.

"Mama!"

"Sarah, you just... you bumped it." Jake righted the tablet and aimed it so that Natalie and Baojia could see their little faces. "Did I do it? Can you see us?"

Natalie felt like she couldn't breathe even though she didn't need to. It was a weird feeling. She nodded and knew she was crying.

"Hey guys." Baojia was smiling. "We miss you so much. Have you been being good for Giovanni and B?"

Natalie swallowed the lump in her throat and focused on Baojia's hand rubbing her back. "Hey, baby." She touched the screen by Jake's face and was startled when it went wavy. "Oh sh— Bugger. Oh bugger."

"Careful." Baojia moved her hand away. "Just the edges. You can touch the edges." He kept rubbing her back.

"Mama, why are you crying?" Sarah was already

climbing on the back of the couch. "I miss you. I went to the barn today with Dema and Andre and I saw kittens."

"I miss you too." She wiped her eyes, hiding the red-stained tissue in her hand. "Tell me about the kittens."

Sarah blathered about the kittens for a few minutes, and Jake stared at her silently.

"Hey, Jakey." She smiled at his solemn little face.

"Are you okay?" he asked.

"I'm more than okay. I promise. Dad is with me, and Uncle Lucien and Auntie Mak. I promise I'm okay."

"You're crying."

She shrugged. "I'm just emotional, and I miss you, buddy."

Baojia leaned over and kissed her temple. "I promise I'm taking good care of her. She's doing great."

Jake's eyes lit up. "Are you drinking blood now? Like Dad?"

Natalie laughed a little. "Yeah, but you want to hear something weird?"

"What?"

She whispered, "I actually like cow blood best."

Jake wrinkled his nose. "No way."

"Yes way. Really. I'm a superweird vampire, I think."

Natalie had been both bothered and relieved to learn that cow blood satisfied her as much or more than human blood. She still drank her share of human blood—Lucien's orders—but while that tasted overly rich after the first few swallows, cow blood tasted great. Everyone thought she was nuts except Carwyn.

Carwyn—upon hearing about her preference for cow blood over human—automatically assumed they were distantly related, citing her freckles, red hair, and superior intelligence.

Natalie found nothing in that to dispute.

"Tell me what you've been doing while I've been gone," Natalie said. "Sarah, don't crawl on the back of the couch like that please."

"Isabel says it's okay!"

"Did I just ask you not to do it?" Natalie asked. "Please listen, because I'm not going to say it again."

Baojia hugged her from the side. "Some things don't change."

"Just because I'm not there doesn't mean—"

"Oh!" Jake interjected as Sarah was climbing back down to her seat. "Mom, can we see your fangs?"

"Oh!" Sarah bounced up and down. "Let me see, let me see!"

"Told you," Baojia muttered.

Natalie felt weirder than she had in weeks. "Uh... Sarah, stop bouncing on the furniture and I'll show you my fangs."

Sarah stopped bouncing immediately. Both kids leaned into the camera until all Natalie could see were the tops of their heads.

"Okay." She swallowed hard and tried to will her fangs to come down. "Okay, I'm still figuring all this out, so—"

Baojia ran a finger along the inside of her thigh, and her fangs popped down immediately.

"Whoa! So cool!"

"I like them, Mama! You have nice fangs. They look really sharp."

"Uh-huh." She gave Baojia a dirty look, but he was biting back a laugh. "Thanths, guyth."

Sarah put a hand over her mouth and giggled. "You talk funny now."

Jake was smiling too. "That's so weird, Mom."

"Thanks." She swallowed hard and stretched her mouth until her fangs retreated. "I'm still getting the hang of it. Glad to know I'm weird."

"The weirdest." Jake's eyes were dancing, just like his father's. "Miss you, Mom."

"I miss you too."

Six months later...

Baojia opened the front door just as Natalie threw her notebook against the wall and screamed into a pillow.

"Gaaaaah!"

He raised an eyebrow. "Kids are good, thanks for asking. Isabel says hi and she thinks Adriana would make a great nanny. They're going to call her tonight to see if she can come down and meet us."

"That is great news!" Natalie threw down the pillow and stalked toward him. "This is driving me crazy."

"What is?" For the most part, she'd been adjusting adequately. She still didn't trust herself to be around humans, which showed she had good judgment, but she was venturing more and more outside, so she wasn't in danger of becoming a hermit.

"Tommy keeps emailing me these leads. This is the second one in as many weeks. And I know there's a story here that connects with the Ostenhouse case—"

"That was the trafficking one last year, right?"

"Yes! But remember there was the one guy…" She snapped her fingers. "Yukov. Lukov, something like that…"

"Sokolov?"

"Yes! That guy. And SFPD could never find enough evidence to get the DA to charge him, and then he's international, right? So he walks."

"And disappears." Baojia sat on the edge of the couch. "I heard about him somewhere in Belarus, but after that—"

"He disappears." She threw up her hands. "Poof. And now I'm hearing that there are girls on the East Coast who are disappearing with the same MO. The exact same MO, Baojia. And I can't do anything about it."

"Modeling website?"

"Yep." She paced around the room.

"Sixteen- to eighteen-year-old girls?"

"Three so far. New Jersey, Boston, now New York."

"Diverse racial targets, but all low-income and high achieving?"

"Yes and yes." She picked up the notebook and stalked over to him. "This newest one is seventeen. She was accepted to the magnet high school for music and arts. Superhard to get into. Pretty girl. *Gorgeous* girl. Dominican-American. She's acting weird, mom puts it down to being stressed about starting at the new school. Then she disappears last week. No sign of her. Police are convinced she ran away with her boyfriend, but guess what?"

"She and the boyfriend were already broken up." Baojia stood.

Natalie snapped her fingers. "Exactly. Mom is telling

the police that this isn't like her daughter, and no one is listening."

"Friends?"

"Friends say the girl and the boyfriend broke up because she was approached by—get this—"

"A modeling scout?"

She pointed at him. "Right in one. Boyfriend didn't trust the guy. Girl said he was overreacting and being jealous and it was a good way to earn some extra money. Blah blah blah, she breaks up with him. Friends say she was upset, and they thought it was about the boy, but what if—"

"What if they'd already taken pictures?" Baojia let out a long breath. "Filmed her when she was changing and were blackmailing her?"

"Sounds familiar, right?"

The trafficking ring in San Francisco had done exactly that. They'd targeted bright, pretty girls with promising futures but not a lot of family resources and then lured them into "modeling photo shoots" where they were filmed in the dressing room and it was edited to make it look like amateur pornography. Natalie had worked tirelessly on the story and gotten massive credit by both the investigative-journalism community and law enforcement for information that led to multiple arrests and the rescue of more than a dozen girls.

He walked over to her and put his hands on his shoulders. "Natalie, you can't help with this case."

"But I know what questions to ask." Her eyes pleaded with him. "I don't know New York, but I know the pattern. I know—"

"You are a six-month-old vampire," he said. "Setting

you down in the middle of New York would be like letting a fox loose in a henhouse. And yes, Red, in this situation, you're definitely the fox and not the chicken."

"But I don't even like human blood! It smells like liver and nobody likes liver except cranky old men and I'm not a cranky old man!"

"Natalie, there's no way. You have to drop this. And tell Tommy to stop sending you stuff, okay? It's just going to drive you crazy because you can't do anything about it." He saw the guilty look on her face. "You told him to dig for more, didn't you?"

She mumbled, "Just… reaching out to some people he knows at the *Times*."

Baojia sighed. "You *can't* leave. It's not even a possibility, so just stop tormenting yourself."

"But these girls are out there! They don't kill them. They keep them and they just…" Natalie's face was stricken. "You know what they're doing to them right now. You know it. Is there anything you can do?"

"I can't help like I did back home. It's not my jurisdiction, and no one would appreciate me barging in. The O'Briens rule New York, and unless this is something encroaching on one of their businesses, they do not get involved in human issues. Plus you and the kids are my priority right now. I can't just up and leave."

"But—"

"Out of the question, Natalie. I'm not leaving you, Sarah, and Jake."

She took a deep breath. "But you know people in New York. Ben—"

"Is still in Mongolia, remember? He's in the same boat as you."

"Tenzin?"

Baojia shrugged. "Who knows? And she wouldn't be able to work a case like this anyway. Not without Ben. She'd fly off the handle and just kill everyone."

Natalie cocked her head. "Well…"

"Wow, those shady vampire ethics sure sprang up quick." He grimaced. "Do *not* call Tenzin."

"We have to do something," Natalie said. "The kids are here and we're all fine. Lucien and Makeda have taken care of everything back home. We're just sitting here waiting and—"

"Brigid." Baojia knew it was right the moment he said it. "If you can't leave it up to human law enforcement—"

"They've already written these three girls off as runaways. They're not going to do anything until more and more disappear."

"Then call Carwyn and Brigid. They have resources. Brigid has the skill set, and Carwyn has the connections. She regularly contracts out at this point anyway because Dublin is a sea of calm. No one wants to mess with Murphy when he's the only one who's figured out how to get vampires into the twenty-first century."

She reached up, pulled his face down, and kissed him. "You're brilliant."

"I know." He patted her butt. "Call Brigid. I think she and Carwyn might even be in Los Angeles right now since they finished up that thing for his daughter. This sounds like something they could jump on."

Natalie sped over to her Nocht-enabled tablet and began barking commands at Cara while Baojia went into the kitchen to grab a drink.

Yep, she was exactly the same woman he fell in love

with. Exactly the same heart and passion. Exactly the same drive and exactly the same infuriating lack of self-preservation.

Fortunately, she was now a little bit more durable.

THE END

AFTERWORD

Dear Readers,

Thanks for returning to the Elemental World series. I've been waiting for six years to write the finale of Natalie and Baojia's story, and I'm thrilled to finally answer lingering questions for readers about their lives together.

What's next for the Elemental World? It's hard to say right now. Clearly, though the Elixir storyline has wrapped up, there are still many characters I could feature in future books. So while I will never shut the door on this series, I'll be focusing on two major projects in 2020. I dropped an Easter egg or two in **Valley of the Shadow**, so you might already know what I'm going to say.

1. First up, the last two books of the Elemental Legacy series featuring Ben and Tenzin. **Dawn Caravan** will be coming in April 2020, and the

fifth and final book in the series will hopefully be published toward the end of the year.

2. I will be starting a new, fast-paced, action packed, and brightly patterned paranormal mystery series featuring two of my favorite characters in the Elemental World… Carwyn and Brigid. Did you guess???

That's right, Carwyn and Brigid will be exploring more of the Elemental universe in a brand new series featuring the two of them and many other favorite characters, along with a few new people along the way. There will be fighting. There will be kissing. There will be crime-fighting. And there will be Hawaiian shirts and professional wrestling. OF COURSE. I don't have a title or release date for the series yet, but I'm excited to start writing next year.

I hope you take the time to sign up for my newsletter so you can keep up with all the news about my books. You'll receive a free short story, news about new releases and sales, and a monthly newsletter with free serial fiction starting in January 2020. If you want to keep up with me but don't want extra emails, you can subscribe to my blog at ElizabethHunterWrites.com.

Thanks for reading,
Elizabeth Hunter

Sign up for Elizabeth Hunter's Monthly Newsletter and receive free serial fiction, along with updates about new releases and promotions.

STARTING JANUARY 2020
An all new story in the Cambio Springs Mysteries:
Dᴜsᴛ Bᴏʀɴ

Sean Quinn returned to Cambio Springs to help his family find their way out of trouble. Of course, Quinns were known for causing trouble in the desert town of shapeshifters. But before he can hit the road again, a new threat emerges on the border of his family home, a threat that could leave Sean stuck in the Springs just when he's most desperate to leave.

And one unsuspecting human might be stuck right there with him.

Ever since Juniper Hawkins came to Cambio Springs to visit her big brother, strange things keep happening, not the least was finding the man who'd almost made her change her wandering ways. Juni wasn't the kind of woman who settled down, even when the object of her affection was a tall, dark, and handsome photographer who kissed her senseless then left her in Southeast Asia.

Not that she was still irritated about that.

DUST BORN is a serial novel in the Cambio Springs Mysteries, a paranormal romance series by USA Today Bestselling author, Elizabeth Hunter.

To subscribe to Elizabeth's newsletter, please visit ElizabethHunterWrites.com for more information.

Pulse-pounding paranormal mystery featuring your favorite characters from the Elemental World.

Obsidian's Edge
is now available at all major retailers!

For the first time ever, all three origin novellas in the Elemental Legacy series are available in one volume, along with a bonus novella, *The Bronze Blade*.

In **Shadows and Gold**, driving a truck full of rotting vegetables and twenty million in gold across mainland China wasn't what Ben Vecchio had in mind for summer vacation. If he can keep Tenzin's treasure safe, the reward will be worth the effort. But when has travel with a five-thousand-year-old wind vampire ever been simple?

In **Imitation and Alchemy**, all Ben wanted was a quiet summer before his last semester of university. All Tenzin wanted was a cache of priceless medieval coins that had been missing for several hundred years. And some company.

In **Omens and Artifacts**, Ben needs a job. A *legendary* job. Finding the lost sword of Brennus the Celt would make his reputation in the vampire world, but it could also draw dangerous attention. The Raven King's gold isn't famous for being easy to find. Luckily, Ben has his own legend at his side.

OBSIDIAN'S EDGE is an anthology of novellas in the Elemental Legacy series by Elizabeth Hunter, USA Today Bestselling Author of *Midnight Labyrinth*, *Blood Apprentice*, and other works of fiction.

He's a human in a vampire's world,
but she's the reason he's not sleeping at night.

MIDNIGHT LABYRINTH

Benjamin Vecchio escaped a chaotic childhood and grew to adulthood under the protection and training of one of the Elemental world's most feared vampire assassins. He's traveled the world and battled immortal enemies.

But everyone has to go home sometime.

New York means new opportunities and allies for Ben and his vampire partner, Tenzin. It also means new politics and new threats. Their antiquities business is taking off, and their client list is growing. When Ben is challenged to find a painting lost since the Second World War, he jumps at the chance. This job will keep him closer to home, but it might just land him in hot water with the insular clan of earth vampires who run Manhattan.

Tenzin knew the painting would be trouble before she laid eyes on it, but she can't deny the challenge intrigues her. Human laws mean little to a vampire with a few millennia behind her, and Tenzin misses the rush of taking what isn't hers.

But nothing is more dangerous than a human with half the story, and Ben and Tenzin might end up risking their reputations and their lives before they escape the Midnight Labyrinth.

MIDNIGHT LABYRINTH is the first full length novel in an all-new contemporary fantasy series by Elizabeth

Hunter, author of the Elemental Mysteries and the Irin Chronicles.

If you're a human in a vampire's world,
nothing goes according to plan.

BLOOD APPRENTICE

When a map to the mysterious fortune of notorious privateer Miguel Enríquez falls in the lap of Ben and Tenzin, only one of them is jumping at the opportunity. Tenzin can't wait to search for a secret cache of gold. Ben, on the other hand, couldn't be less excited.

All Ben knows about Puerto Rico is what he hears on the news and a few lingering memories of his human grandmother. Going back to his roots holds zero appeal for the carefully constructed man he's become.

But in the end, the lure of hidden gold can't be denied.

Ben and Tenzin head to Puerto Rico where the immortal world is ruled by *Los Tres*, a trio of powerful vampires commanding the wind, the waves, and the mountains that make up their small island in the Caribbean.

To find Enríquez's treasure, they'll have to walk a fine line between flattery and secrecy. To leave the island might mean a bigger fight than either one of them foresaw.

Blood Apprentice is the second novel in the Elemental Legacy, a paranormal mystery series by Elizabeth Hunter, author of the Irin Chronicles.

Sometimes falling is the safest step to take.

THE DEVIL AND THE DANCER

Chloe Reardon has a problem, and his name is Gavin Wallace.

Okay, Gavin isn't exactly a problem, unless you consider a highly attractive wind vampire with dubious intentions a problem. Especially if that vampire is your boss. With an affinity for kilts and excellent taste in music.

But none of that matters because Chloe Reardon has had enough of dangerous men. Danger is overrated. Danger is the opposite of sexy. So Gavin is the last man— or vampire—on earth she needs to let into her heart.

Except what if the most dangerous man you knew was also the one who made you feel the strongest?

The Devil and the Dancer is a paranormal romance novella in the Elemental Legacy series.

Darkness comes for everyone,
and some fates are inescapable.

NIGHT'S RECKONING

For over a thousand years, the legendary sword Laylat al Hisab—the Night's Reckoning—has been lost in the waters of the East China Sea. Forged as a peace offering between two ancient vampires, the sword has eluded treasure hunters, human and immortal alike.

But in time, even the deep gives up its secrets.

When Tenzin's sire hears about the ninth century shipwreck found off the coast of southern China, Zhang Guo realizes he'll need the help of an upstart pirate from Shanghai to retrieve it. And since that pirate has no desire to be in the middle of an ancient war, Cheng calls the only allies who might be able to help him avoid it.

Unfortunately, Tenzin is on one side of the globe and Ben is on the other.

Tenzin knows she'll need Ben's keen mind and political skills to complete the job. She also knows gaining Ben's cooperation won't be an easy task. She'll have to drag him back into the darkness he's been avoiding.

Whether Ben knows it or not, his fate is balanced on the edge of a thousand-year-old blade, and one stumble could break everything Tenzin has worked toward.

Night's Reckoning is the third novel in the Elemental Legacy series, a paranormal mystery by Elizabeth Hunter, USA Today bestselling author of the Elemental Mysteries.

COMING SPRING 2020
DAWN CARAVAN
Elemental Legacy Book Four

Please subscribe to my newsletter for more information about the Elemental Legacy series and other news and updates about my books.

ACKNOWLEDGMENTS

This year has been a whirlwind. There has been hard stuff, fun stuff, and lots of work. I have published four novels and two novellas. I have visited a brand new country and started a brand new series. I have met goats, zebras, and an elephant named Tail-less.

And through it all, my family has been my rock. I could not have survived this year without my husband and my son, who are both amazing and loving guys. D, I am so proud to be your wife. C, I am so proud to be your mom.

I also could not have made it through without the team of professionals who make this all possible. I want to first thank my two assistants, Gen and Jenn, who make life happen and make sure all the posts get posted and the bills get paid so I can focus on writing.

I want to thank Amy Cissell, my extraordinary content editor, and Anne Victory, my line editor, with additional thanks to Linda at Victory Editing. These three amazing pros make my writing shine, and I could not do this without them.

To my agents, Jane Dystel and Lauren Abramo, thank you for everything. To my publicity team at Social Butterfly PR, thank you for your hard work and attention.

To my cover artists at Damonza.com, I thank you for your professionalism and vision for my books.

To my reader group, Hunters' Haven, I want to send special thanks, especially to the admins, Meg, Hannah, Danielle, Tiffany, and Fiona.

And to my readers around the world, thank you forever for your support.

Here's to a healthy and happy 2020!

ABOUT THE AUTHOR

ELIZABETH HUNTER is a *USA Today* and international best-selling author of romance, contemporary fantasy, and paranormal mystery. Based in Central California, she travels extensively to write fantasy fiction exploring world mythologies, history, and the universal bonds of love, friendship, and family. She has published over thirty works of fiction and sold over a million books worldwide. She is the author of Love Stories on 7th and Main, the Elemental Legacy series, the Irin Chronicles, the Cambio Springs Mysteries, and other works of fiction.

ElizabethHunterWrites.com

The Bronze Blade

The Scarlet Deep

A Very Proper Monster

A Stone-Kissed Sea

Valley of the Shadow

The Irin Chronicles

The Scribe

The Singer

The Secret

The Staff and the Blade

The Silent

The Storm

The Seeker

The Cambio Springs Series

Long Ride Home

Shifting Dreams

Five Mornings

Desert Bound

Waking Hearts

Contemporary Romance

The Genius and the Muse

7th and Main

INK

HOOKED

GRIT

Linx & Bogie Mysteries

A Ghost in the Glamour

A Bogie in the Boat

Made in the USA
Las Vegas, NV
20 March 2024